# BETRAYAL

I0626642

## LOLA
## TAYLOR

**The third book in the smoldering, romantic series featuring a whole lot of fur and a whole lot of curves.**

If it's not one thing, it's another. Gage's worst fears have come to light. One of his own has betrayed him, nearly resulting in the death of his mate. Then he finds out the betrayer was in league with the High King of werewolves, the man who took out the hit for unknown reasons. When Alara, the king's illegitimate daughter—and his brother's new mate—elects Gage as a contender for the crown, he's torn between duty and love once more. On one hand, becoming High King could allow him to get closer to the witch who's pulling the strings—the mysterious Mistress Black. On the other hand, it almost certainly means putting his mate that much closer to danger.

And Gage isn't the only one who's after the crown. Werewolves of all backgrounds rise up to put their chips into play in what becomes one of the deadliest power struggles in werewolf history. The stakes are higher than ever, especially when a foe from Gage's past shows up with the sole intention of making Danica his.

If their love is to survive, Danica and Gage will have to work together to uncover the true motives behind the witch mafia's activity and defeat the most wicked enemy either of them has ever known. Secrets will be revealed, love will be tested, and ghosts from the past will emerge in this third exciting installment to the sexy Blood Moon Rising series.

*Betrayal*
First Edition © 2014 Lola Taylor
Third Edition © 2016 Lola Taylor

Cover designed by Kitten of Deranged Doctor Design
Interior design and formatting by Champagne Formats
Editing by Jen of Mistress Editing
Indigo Dreamer Press logo designed by Indi99o of 99designs
Author photograph by Sara Rogers Photography

www.lolataylorbooks.com
www.indigodreamerpress.com

ISBN-10: 0-9981140-0-6
ISBN-13: 978-0-9981140-0-2

For more information, please visit
www.lolataylorbooks.com

# CHAPTER ONE

ANICA HAD ONLY A FEW SECONDS BEFORE HER MATE'S emotions slammed into her, the heaviest of which was shock. The sheer force of it, coupled with her own swirling feelings, held her body immobile while her mind raced to process what Alara had just said.

*"I want to name you my successor."*

Alara wanted Gage to be High King of the werewolves. And that would make Danica....

Her heart began to race, rocketing from moderate to oh-my-God. She'd only recently grown accustomed to the idea of ruling a pack. Now Alara thought Danica could rule an entire nation of werewolves? Was she insane? Danica fit in with the royal crowd as much as a wolf did among sheep, no pun intended.

The silence between the four wolves stretched uncomfortably.

Danica tasted Gage's feelings through their bond as he

recovered, which was apparently one of the weird side effects of mating to another werewolf. It gave the term "soul mates" new meaning. The vibrant tang of shock briefly gave way to sweet hope and then quickly soured with fear.

"I can't," Gage said, his face as hard as stone.

"Brother," Nik said carefully, taking a step toward him, "I know she's springing this on you out of the blue, but I think you should take a moment to consider what she's offering. Think of the good you could do."

"Think of the damage," Gage replied without hesitation. Danica sensed his growing bitterness and terror along with a heaping of self-loathing that made her heart ache for him. "In case you have forgotten, I single-handedly managed to slaughter a good number of my pack in one fell swoop only a short while after claiming the rank of Alpha. Even Malachite would be impressed."

"Bullshit," Nik spat. "Malachite's done far worse, and we both know it. Don't even pretend for a second you're anything like that piece of shit."

"But what if I am?" Gage countered, his voice growing louder. He shook his head, at a brief loss for words. "After everything we've been through with Malachite, I vowed never to subject my pack to that kind of mindless violence again. But I can feel it." He stared at the trembling fist at his side. "I can feel my bloodlust surge when I'm in wolf form. I crave the taste of flesh and the snapping of bones. And I fear someday I won't be able to control the wolf and it will consume me. Anyone near me will pay the price."

Nik ran a hand through his hair. "You're being paranoid."

"Nik," Alara chastised quietly.

"I'm being careful," Gage said sternly, ignoring the insult. "Carnage is in our blood, Nik. Father made sure of that."

They held each other's eyes a long while, something unreadable passing between them. It was selfish to feel jealous of the bond between them, which in turn made her feel guilty, but she couldn't help it. She hadn't pressed Gage to open up about his family, aside from the CliffsNotes version he'd already relayed to her. Some hurts were best left alone. Otherwise, the wounds would never heal.

"Listen, little bro," Nik said, stepping forward and gripping Gage's shoulders, "how long are you going to hold on to your loathing of our father?"

"Jesus, Nik, I don't loathe him." Gage stepped away and pinched the bridge of his nose. With a frustrated sigh, he dropped his hand. "I don't know how I feel about him."

Nik gazed at his brother with concern and sympathy. "Look, whatever it is that's holding you back from running for High King, don't be afraid to face it. That's all I'm saying."

Gage didn't say anything as he looked away, signaling the end of the conversation.

Danica sensed his urge to run and placed a hand on his arm. "Why don't we head back to our room and let them get cleaned up before the meeting tonight?"

"Good idea," Alara said, quickly catching on. "The meeting starts in an hour, and regardless of what you decide, as an Alpha you should be there."

Gage gave her a curt nod.

"We'll be by in a half hour to pick you up," Alara said, stepping aside so they could walk out.

Nik had his arms crossed, a worried frown plastered on his face as he watched Gage head past them toward the door like he couldn't escape fast enough.

Not wanting to leave on an awkward foot, Danica paused and smiled. "Congratulations again, you two."

Alara smiled back, and that excited sparkle returned to Nik's eyes as he kissed his new mate's neck.

Danica left and softly shut the door behind her, finding her mate waiting for her in the hallway.

He leaned with his back against the wall, his arms crossed and a brooding expression on his face.

"Careful," Danica said, gently pressing the tip of her nail into his cheek. "My aunt said if you frown too much, your face will get stuck that way."

Gage blinked a few times as his eyes focused on her. "I'm sorry, love. What did you say?"

Danica sighed and grabbed his arm. "Come on, you. Let's walk."

They strode alongside each other in silence for a ways. Their room was over in the next wing, which, needless to say, was quite a walk from here. Normally she would have spent the time admiring the extravagance around them, but all she could look at was Gage. When Danica couldn't stand the silence any longer, she said, "How are you handling all this?"

*"Let's use our bond to talk,"* Gage said through their telepathic pack link. *"Too many prying wolf ears in one place for my liking."*

"*Oh. Gotcha.*" She still didn't want to talk through her mind by default, at least, not like Gage, Nik, and other longtime werewolves. It was yet another bizarre aspect about her new life that was starting to sink in as a reality but wasn't quite concrete yet.

"*To answer your question,*" Gage went on, "*I don't know.*"

Danica waited, trying to think of a way to wheedle some clarification out of him.

"*What about you?*" he asked. "*How would you feel about being High Queen?*"

Her heart sped up, and her palms went clammy. "*I could handle it.*"

"*Danica....*"

"*All right, all right, it scares the bejesus out of me. I just don't want my fears to get in the way of you making the decision that's best for you.*" She squeezed his hand. "*I'll support whatever you decide.*"

They stopped in front of their door, the conversation pausing as Gage unlocked it. Once inside, he said aloud, "See, that's the problem. I can't risk exposing you."

"What are you talking about?"

"I'm talking about how there was a hit on you—could still be, for all we know—and Alara's wanting to drag us into the spotlight. We might as well attach a neon sign to you!"

"Gage—"

He cupped her face in his hands, making her breath catch. "And there is no way in hell I can be moved to ever place you in danger again. I don't care what's at stake. The whole damned world could be falling apart, and even if sacrificing you was the only way to save it, I'd hold you tight and watch the world burn."

Danica searched his eyes. All she saw was desperation. And fear. Cold, soul-corroding fear.

Taking his hands, she twined her fingers with his. She thought through what she wanted to say before she spoke. "I know you think I'm still this breakable human, but I'm not." Determination hardened her features, and she straightened her spine. "I'm stronger than you think. Don't underestimate me."

"I would never be so foolish, dearest." He kissed her forehead and then rested his cheek against her curls. "I just can't stand to lose you too."

Just like his father, mother, his older brother, his pack-mates…. Gage had suffered so much loss in his life. So had she, to be honest. Her whole family had literally vanished over the years, leaving her alone in the world.

Save for Gage. In the end, when it was all said and done, they had each other.

Danica freed her hands and wrapped her arms around him. "I'm not going anywhere."

"Good. Because I don't intend on ever letting you go. Werewolves tend to be possessive, especially Alphas."

"Good," she murmured with a smile of contentment. "Possess me all you want."

They stayed like that a few moments, holding each other and listening to one another's hearts beat. Since becoming an Alpha's mate, Danica hadn't gotten to spend much alone time with him. There was always something that needed to be done, some political treaty to look over, or a charity ball for supernaturals…. Being an Alpha's mate was no different from being the mayor's wife. Honestly, she didn't know what she had been expecting. Fantastic sex at all hours of the day while they frolicked in the moonlight as wolves at night?

Thinking of moonlight made her skin tingle with that familiar itch she'd felt all afternoon. Her eyes flicked to the pale silver light spilling through the lace curtains of their balcony.

Gage followed her gaze. "You feel it calling to you, don't you?" he murmured.

"Yes," she said without hesitation, still transfixed by the moonlight. "It's been just like you said it would. I feel like I could go through a whole bottle of anti-itch cream and it wouldn't be enough."

He chuckled, the deep sound rolling through her chest and setting her more at ease. He rubbed her arms reassuringly. "The Change is… well, let's just say it's an 'out-of-body experience.'"

"Ha ha," she said wryly, tacking a smile on at the end.

Her heart pounded just thinking about her bones shifting into something else, something wilder.

Freer.

Thank God both the Change and the mating ceremony couldn't take place on the same full moon. Having sex for the first time with her mate, and in front of their pack, no less, had been nerve-wracking enough. Turning into another creature altogether was in a totally different category of weird.

"Don't worry," Gage said. He took her hand and squeezed, running the rough pad of his thumb over the smooth skin along the back of her knuckles. "I'll be there the whole time to guide you through it."

Danica smiled up at him as confidently as she could, though her stomach still did somersaults that made her want to regurgitate her dinner.

A moment of silence passed, and Danica looked up to find her mate watching her with a wry smile.

"What?" she said.

He grinned and pulled her toward the bed. "Come away from the window before you start howling."

She playfully nudged him and he tucked her in beside him on top of the bed. Finally tearing her eyes from the moonlight, she leaned her head against his chest and said softly, "What do you think you're going to do about running for High King? Nik and Alara will be here soon."

Gage was silent a moment and then he sighed hard. "I'm going to decline it."

"What?" Danica abruptly sat up and stared down at him. "Why?"

Emotion swam in his eyes as he toyed with a curl of hers. "I have to protect you at any cost."

"Gage, love"—she took his hand and kissed his fingers—"I'm not going to lie that becoming High Queen intimidates me. Hell, I'm still getting used to being the mate of an Alpha in a minor pack. But I can also sense how innately good you are." She rested her hand over his chest, right where his heart was. "I've discovered that part of being mated to someone is knowing the color of their soul, and yours is so pure it puts mine to shame. At the summit, those people…." She shivered just thinking about it. "Not one of those Alphas possessed a tenth of caring and genuine kindness that you do. And as much as being queen frightens me, it scares me even more to think what would happen to our kind if one of them became High King."

She cupped his face and stared intently into his eyes. "You can't go down without a fight, even if you're scared. We're all scared of something, whether we admit to it or not. It's what keeps us human. And I know you feel like you've been alone, because I can feel your loneliness like it's carved a hole in my own chest. But you don't have to be so strong and stubborn all the time. We're in this together. Come hell or high water, I'm going to be here for you no matter what we face. So what if being king scares you? You're Gage Johnson, an Alpha werewolf. You're strong enough to do this, and I'm strong enough to stand by your side."

He went silent, searching her eyes. "Danica—"

"Sssh." She placed a finger to his lips. "You don't have to decide right this minute. Just think about it, okay?"

He nodded once, and she resettled against his chest. For several silent minutes they lay there, lost in their own thoughts.

Danica pressed her lips together, unsure whether the indecision she felt was hers or Gage's. Sometimes the tangle of emotions was downright maddening.

A knock came at the door.

Gage sighed and they sat up together. "That's Nik."

"Yeah." She smiled. "Go kick some ass, tiger."

The corners of his mouth pulled up into that sexy grin she'd first fallen for back at the bar. "Wouldn't it be more appropriate to say *wolf*?"

She wrapped her arms around his neck and smiled against his lips. "Maybe."

As they kissed, impatient knocking came from the door. "Gage, get your ass out here."

They reluctantly parted, and Gage stood, straightening his collared shirt and wiping away her lipstick with a tissue. "We both know patience isn't Nik's strong suit," he said with a wink. "I'll be back for your first Change. See you soon."

"Good luck," Danica said, smiling. "No matter what you decide, I'll be here."

His eyes warmed. He nodded and then left with Nik and Alara.

Once alone, Danica fell back against the sheets with a huge sigh. Instinctively, her head turned toward the window.

Gage told her that werewolf magic—which stemmed from the curse that allowed them to shift—actually came from nature, and thus, was a type of Green Magic. From this point forward, she'd crave to be outdoors as her inner wolf was constantly drawn to the open sky and fresh air. She'd already craved that long before she'd been marked. Sunshine, lush green grass, and a vibrant blue sky were much more preferable than the dark, gloomy shack she'd lived in as a human. More than anything, that place had served as a reminder of how alone she was and that everyone had abandoned her.

Blinking away the memories of her dark past, she looked away from the moon and wondered about the prospect of living here if she became queen. The castle was beautiful, but did she really want this life? Having been the mate of an ordinary Alpha for only a month, she knew better than to think the strain of all their responsibilities would lift if they moved up the social ladder. If anything, the duties piled upon them would grow.

Would their relationship eventually snap under the weight and added pressure? Since werewolf couples technically weren't married, they couldn't divorce if things went south.

Sadness wrenched her heart, and she firmly shoved that depressing thought away. Losing Gage was something she most certainly did not want to think about.

Standing, she walked about the room and ran her fingers over the fine furniture and expensive items before looking out the window again.

Their suite was high up on the third floor. The forest lay below her, the tips of the trees dusted in moonlight. Several yards away, a lake shimmered like diamonds.

She imagined what she'd look like up here from the perspective of someone driving up to the castle—like a dot, a speck, or a ghost even. *More like a princess locked away in a tower.* Before she'd met Gage, all she'd ever wanted was to escape her old life. What if this new one caged her in just as much as her human life had? She'd been bound to a day job she'd loathed because she couldn't find a better job that would give her enough money to pay her bills, and even then, those were so high she could barely afford the cost of living. Now she'd have to push aside her own wants because of her title within the werewolf community.

Danica leaned her head against the cool glass and sighed. When she was a little girl, she'd always dreamed of being a princess. She'd never considered what exactly that entailed. There was so much more to it than pretty dresses and living her happily-ever-after. But of course, fairy tales never got into the nitty-gritty of real-life problems.

Danica couldn't help letting her mind wander....

What if the princess had started to feel trapped? What if eventually the castle became a prison and the crown her shackles?

Could she still bring herself to love the prince who had brought her there, or would she grow to resent him?

Would she still be free to live her own life on her own terms? Or would she forever be defined by the crown she wore while the person she was beneath the dress slowly vanished until she was forgotten?

# CHAPTER TWO

As he followed Alara and Nik down the hall, Gage's mind flipped back and forth between two things: Danica's well-being and the realization he could very well inherit the throne.

To even consider becoming High King was ludicrous.

Immediately, thoughts of all the danger he'd be putting Danica in plagued his mind, and it made him sick to his stomach. The thought of losing her filled him with despair, like the moment he realized his father, his mother, and his eldest brother were never coming back to him. It filled him with a coldness that penetrated his bones.

His jaw ticked as he walked behind his brother and Alara. When he made the decision to fight Malachite for the right to rule the Moonstruck Pack, it had been an easy choice because all he could think about was protecting his pack. But the position of High King presented so many more complications. He would no longer be responsible for the well-being of a single pack, but rather that of several hundred. It would be up to him and his queen to keep the peace between the werewolves and the other supernatural races. If war broke out, it would be on his head. If one little thing went wrong, people would despise him, and werewolves tended to hold grudges.

If he became High King, he would have his paws full. It made Gage sick with worry just thinking about all the aspects of his world that could stand for improvement. Things would have to change in order to better the werewolf race as a whole, and Gage could think of more than a few Alphas with deep pockets who wouldn't like those changes because it would hurt their corrupt businesses. People would come after him.

And Danica.

"Gage?"

He was so lost in thought that he nearly slammed into Alara, who'd stopped, but Nik grabbed his arm and diverted his direction at the last minute.

"Easy there," Nik said. "You're going to knock out my mate before we've been able to really break in our sheets."

Alara shoved him as Nik chuckled and her face turned as red as her silk dress. Her brown hair was swept into a bun, showing off her new tattoos. The swirling blue lines crawled over her shoulders and down her back. She looked stunning, like a queen should.

For all his vices, her father, King Victor, had at least looked the part of a High King. Gage tried imagining himself as High King and couldn't see anything more than a country boy who still struggled to fill a man's shoes from time to time. Hell, he still hadn't fully adjusted to thinking of himself as the Alpha of a minor pack.

"Listen, Gage," Alara said, interrupting his thoughts. She held his gaze, a question in her eyes. "Before we go in there, I need to know where you stand. I want you to know I won't hold your decision against you. It's yours to make. I will not force the crown on you." Her eyes darkened. "I know all too well what it's like being coerced into something you do not want, and I would never wish that upon anyone."

Gage ran a hand over his face and growled a sigh. "I wish I had an easy answer for you, but I don't. If it were just me, I'd say, 'Hell yes, let's do this.' But Danica…."

Nik wrapped a lazy arm around Alara's shoulders and pulled her small frame into his chest. "I hear you on that one, man. But you've got to remember you're an Alpha now, and no matter what you do, she'll always be in the spotlight somehow. You can't lock her away from the world just because you're scared she'll get hurt—or because you will."

The terror of losing Danica returned, along with a chill worse than death. Feeling haunted by losses he'd already suffered, he said, "I can't lose her too, Nik."

Nik's expression filled with understanding. He nodded once, lips turned upward in a grim smile, and took Alara's hand. "Guess that's that. You'll have to pick another heir."

For the most part, Alara hid her disappointment well. After all, she'd grown up amongst royalty and some of the most cutthroat politicians in the Underworld. Perfecting her poker face was a survival skill.

But when Gage saw how much disappointment filled her lovely eyes, he felt his heart wrench. Letting people down wasn't something he liked to make a habit. But he'd also meant what he'd said to his mate—if he had to choose her welfare or that of his race's, he'd always choose hers, damn the consequences.

"I'm sorry," he said softly.

Alara shook her head and her eyes warmed. "It's all right. I understand. Believe me, I do. Sometimes you have to do what's right for you."

Nik gave him an encouraging nod, and together, the three of them turned the corner.

The meeting chamber was down a long corridor lined with the portraits of all the other previous High Kings.

Gage surveyed them with growing distaste as each king's expression became more arrogant than the last's. How is that the men who cared so little about the common people became their leaders?

*Because money buys power.*

This was exactly why he avoided politics whenever possible. Gage was ready to punch through a wall from frustration by the time they arrived at the meeting room. The murmur of conversation drifted through the cracked doors; from what he could hear, there were mostly men inside.

Alara looked back at her companions. "Ready?"

"To get this over with," Nik muttered, and Gage couldn't agree more. Both of them looked like they'd rather have their souls sucked out by a succubus than walk

16

through those doors.

Alara sighed. "I think I'll have one of the servants fetch us some liquor after this."

Nik squeezed her hand. "It'll be fine. I'll be there the entire time, just a few steps away."

She gave him a tight smile, looking noticeably paler than before.

Gage felt sorry for her. He knew she was nervous about telling everyone she wasn't really the High King's daughter. There was no telling how they would react, especially considering how wound up they already were over the events that had unfolded these past few days.

Alara nodded to the guards. They opened the doors, and out spilled all the overly polite conversations. Heads turned as the trio walked into the room, and the noise gradually died down.

The room was circular and arranged with stadium seating. The room could seat three hundred, and it was nearly filled to capacity. The marble pillars lining the walls stretched all the way to the vaulted ceiling, from which hung a golden chandelier glittering with thousands of bulbs and tiny dangling crystals. Banners bearing the pack crests hung along the wall in rows, representing all four hundred.

Gage spotted Moonstruck's crest near his seat at the front; it was a moon partially eclipsed in darkness, with a pair of daggers that crisscrossed over it.

Gage and Nik exchanged glances, then parted ways as Gage climbed the steps and sidled down the third row to his seat.

Someone whistled nearby, and Gage leaned forward. Down the row were Shawna and Jason, who was waving excitedly while Shawna rolled her eyes.

Gage couldn't help but soften at the sight of the kid and smile back, giving him a brief, friendly wave. It had saddened him more than he thought to feel his pack bond to the pup grow weaker with each passing hour he was mated with Shawna. Though he could barely hear the other werewolf's thoughts since he'd mated with Shawna and thus joined her pack, Gage could imagine what was rolling through the kid's head. The words *epic* and *freaking cool* were probably in there somewhere. Gage would miss him. Jason had already informed him he would be leaving with Shawna to rejoin her pack after this meeting.

Nik remained at the bottom of the stairs and positioned himself alongside a wall near the podium, where Alara stood waiting to address the room.

Gage watched as a tall, elegant Alpha with black hair streaked with gray—Norman Black of the Nightshade Pack—leaned over to Nik and said, "Betas aren't allowed in here."

"I am while my mate's in here." Nik's eyes glowed gold. "Besides"—he let his eyes rove Norman's pompous attire—"I bet I'm more Alpha than you are."

"How dare you!" Norman shrieked, his face red with rage.

"Care to prove me otherwise?" Nik said with a flirt of that bloodthirsty grin he always got before ripping someone to pieces.

"Gentlemen," boomed Alara's regal voice over the

speaker system. She looked pointedly at Nik before returning her gaze to the crowd. "If we're done observing the size of each other's dicks, I suggest we get started."

Nik smirked while Norman scowled.

Gage grinned. *That's my boy.*

Alara gripped the sides of the podium, slowly gazing out over the sea of heads and expectant eyes. Gage could practically hear her heart take flight as her nerves choked her.

At last, she took a shaky breath, which was amplified by the mic. To her credit, her voice only warbled a little when she first spoke; she gained confidence as she went on. "Almost all of you have been packmasters long enough to witness Alphas come and go, but never a High King. This position normally falls to the firstborn child of the ruling family, be that a boy or a girl." She swallowed hard, pausing. "I may be the firstborn, but I am not Victor Crescent's daughter."

Gage tensed as the air was sucked out of the room, leaving a silence so pristine you could practically hear people's hearts beating with anticipation.

Alara's nails dug into the wooden frame of the podium. "It has come to light recently by my father's own confession that the queen, my mother, had an affair, resulting in the pregnancy that brought me to this world." She looked them dead-on. "As such, I am illegitimate and no longer eligible to inherit the crown."

No one breathed. Hundreds of shocked looks were mirrored by the people around Gage, all of whom stared at Alara like she'd just declared she was the Anti-Christ.

Someone dropped their cell phone, and all hell broke loose.

People stood, shouting and arguing, each man or woman yelling about how they would be the best king or queen.

The sound of a gavel striking the stand broke through the noise. "Enough!" Alara snarled into the mic. Her voice boomed through the room, making her sound like an angry goddess.

The whole room froze. Sweet, obedient Alara had never raised her voice in public.

She stood tall behind the podium, eyes blazing gold. "I may not be able to inherit the crown, but I am still my father's daughter, by blood or not. And until someone can be diplomatically selected by the High Council, *I* am your princess. And I command you to *sit. Down*."

Like a bunch of scolded dogs, the Alphas all sat back down in awkward silence. All but one.

"You bastard," the old Alpha spat, striding toward the podium. "You're not worthy of royalty, you mutt!"

No sooner had he spoken the last word did Nik's fist collide with his jaw, toppling him backward and onto his ass with an, "Oomph!"

Nik stood over the man, planting a foot on his chest and growling, "Another word and it will be your last."

Alara came down from the podium and rested a hand on her mate's shoulder. "It's fine. There's no need to harm him." She raised her voice. "Guards."

Silently, the uniformed men came forward, grabbed the scowling Alpha, and hauled him to his feet.

He glared in silent fury at Alara, who kept her features calm and collected.

"Please take Mr….?"

"Go to hell!"

"Please take Mr. 'Go to hell' to his chambers. Childish behavior deserves a time-out."

"You bitch, I'll have you know I come from a long line of—"

Nik didn't hold anything back this time. His fist flew out, striking the Alpha squarely in the temple. His eyes rolled back and he slouched in the guards' arms.

Nik shrugged. "Sorry, boys. Guess you'll be carrying him out."

Alara pinched the bridge of her nose as the guards carted off the sleeping Alpha. "Really? Did you have to knock him out?"

"No one talks shit about my girl." He laid a smooch on her cheek, at which she rolled her eyes.

"Your decorum is going to need some work," she said sternly, though her eyes and the corner of her mouth were slightly smiling.

Nik winked at her as he returned to his post along the wall and she to the podium. After she composed herself, she continued. "Though this has not happened in decades, there is a procedure that shall be carried out to ensure a new king or queen is elected as soon as possible. As you may or may not know, no supernatural race alone chooses its own leaders. A High Council comprised of high-ranking members of each race always selects the leader from a pool of qualified candidates. This is to prevent bias and keep things running peacefully between our races. Any mated Alpha may put his or her name in the hat to be considered, so to speak, and the High Council chooses the best candidate for the crown. Until the time such an heir is elected, I will stand in as regent. There are no laws stating a regent must be of pure royal descent," she said as grumbling started to arise.

"What about the witch mafia?" called out a man from across the hall. "Shouldn't we postpone this until we find out who's behind the attacks?"

People nodded their heads.

"No," Alara said firmly. "Now, we are more vulnerable than ever. Without a leader, the witches have even more incentive to strike at us. We must choose a new leader soon.

"The rules stand as such: A nomination box awaits on a table outside the door. If you are a mated Alpha, you may place your ballot inside the box no later than tomorrow at noon. At that time, the ballots shall be collected and sifted through by the High Council, and nominations will be officially announced." Her expression turned grim. "Guard your mates, ladies and gentlemen. Realize that by placing your name in that box, you risk the lives of those closest to you. It has been ages since a High King or Queen was chosen, a rite surrounded by blood, greed, and betrayal. Mind your surroundings, and as the old adage goes, 'Keep your friends close and your enemies closer.' We shall adjourn until tomorrow at two p.m., when the candidates are announced."

She slammed the gavel down on the podium once

more, dismissing the room. Everyone began to get up, and Gage impatiently made his way down to where Nik and Alara stood.

"That's it?" Gage said. "People can just nominate themselves?"

"Yes," Alara replied simply, a devious smile crossing her red lips. "Why? You reconsidering?"

"…No."

She pointed a finger at him, narrowing her eyes. "I heard a catch."

"It just seems this will take forever if just anybody can pitch their own names," he said, eager to get the topic off him.

"On the contrary, it expedites it, as there are only a handful of mated Alphas."

Gage hadn't thought of that, but it didn't surprise him. It drove home the fact that the statistic was most likely earned from Alphas' mates being targeted for assassination. After all, an unmated Alpha couldn't remain a king or queen of wolves for long.

Which was precisely the reason he would never subject Danica to that.

Still, it frightened him to think of the filth that was already heading to the hall to nominate themselves.

*At this rate, the witches might as well finish us off before some selfish idiot embarrasses the werewolf nation.*

"Someone should put a caution sign on you," Nik said, grinning at Gage. "'Excessive brooding over here. Be careful not to trip on the deep frown.'"

"I was not brooding," Gage growled.

Nik grinned. "Careful, brother. Keep it up and we'll have to buy you more black clothing and stock your classic rock collection with heavy metal and emo rock."

Gage couldn't help but crack a smile.

Alara waggled her brows. "I do believe he's reconsidering."

Gage sighed in exasperation. "For the last time, I am not—"

"I surely hope you're not considering putting in your name. I believe our princess said mated Alphas, not mated pups, may place their ballots in the hat."

Gage gritted his teeth, unable to keep from rolling his eyes. Hadn't he met his asshole quota for one lifetime?

Norman smiled pleasantly at them.

"What the hell do you want?" Nik said, stepping forward to stand beside his brother.

Gage's brows raised. Leave it to Nik to get right to the point, part of his whole "screw decorum while dealing with slimebags" protocol.

The pseudo-insult brushed right off Norman's thousand-dollar suit. "Nothing," he said, smiling wider to reveal his fangs. Most werewolves' teeth were at least a little pointier than humans'. "I was merely walking by and overheard your conversation."

"More like you were eavesdropping," Alara said lightly with just a hint of accusation and more steel than an armored van.

"No, no, no," Norman cooed, "I would never dream of that. I am a gentleman, after all. I don't resort to such petty tactics. Can I help what my ears overhear?"

"I don't know," Nik said, stepping up to Norman so he towered over him, "but I might not be able to help throwing you through a window."

Norman stared up at the taller, bulkier werewolf with contempt. "You dare threaten an Alpha, whelp?"

"It's not so much a threat as a fantasy."

Norman's eyes blazed gold as he raised his hand, his nails already sharpening into claws. "You arrogant—"

"Gentlemen!" Alara dove between them, shoving them apart. Her hands trembled, as did her voice. "I have seen more than enough violence these past few days to last a lifetime. If you please…"

Both instantly stood down, looking sheepish. "Sorry, baby," Nik muttered, kissing her head.

She stiffened, stepped back, and pursed her lips like she'd swallowed a lemon. "There is a new word I'd like for you to add to your vocabulary—'decorum.'"

"Not this again." Nik stiffened. "Is it an offense punishable by death for me to want to show affection for my mate?"

"Not when doing so could make me look weak," she hissed.

"Great." He threw up his arms. "Now I make you look weak."

Gage started shrinking away. "Perhaps I'll go see what Danica is up to…."

It didn't appear they'd heard him. Which was even better for him, since they couldn't convince him to stay if they didn't know he was leaving.

He'd taken about three steps down the hall when a

deep voice from his nightmares said, "It's been a while, my protégé."

Gage tripped, his inner wolf immediately going into the defensive as he whirled.

*No… what is he doing here?*

A tall man wearing a black trench coat that barely fit over his bulging arm muscles lounged against the wall with his arms crossed over his chest. The rest of his ensemble was black, making his pale skin seem even whiter. Coupled with his long, pale-blond hair, which hung freely around his face, he looked every bit the part of a dark knight from a fairy tale.

Or from a nightmare.

Gage bared his canines, barely able to utter the man's name. "Malachite."

His former Alpha shot him a devious smile, his malevolent gaze burning gold for a second. "Miss me?"

It was too much—Alara pressuring him to be king, Danica's safety, seeing Malachite again for the first time since the fight that nearly killed them both.

Before common sense could kick in, he'd formed a fist and charged with a roar of rage.

# CHAPTER THREE

STARING OUT THE WINDOW AND DREAMING ABOUT running around naked in the woods howling wasn't something most people dreamed of, but it was the only thing crossing Danica's mind. The higher the moon rose, the crazier the itch in her skin became. Before she could start licking the moonlit glass, Danica promptly drew the drapes shut and clicked on the TV. She idly flipped through channels of reality show after reality show, looking for something mindless to watch.

A late-night rerun of *Say Yes to the Dress* caught her eye, and she sat up in anticipation. Wedding shows— along with cake decorating and haunted houses documentaries—were a guilty obsession of hers. Trashy as it could be some times, reality TV and romance and fantasy novels were her only ways of escaping reality when she lived by herself.

Danica watched with rapt attention as the bride-to-be

modeled dress after expensive dress. Longing swelled in her chest. Cliché as it sounded, since Danica was a little girl, she'd always dreamed of being swept off her feet and having some big dream wedding someday. Now it really did seem like that—a dream. She and Gage had never talked about having a wedding, but part of that might have been because he was super-stressed dealing with pack stuff, and she felt guilty for what seemed like a trivial matter in comparison.

Okay, she knew it wasn't *wrong*, exactly, to want an official wedding. She just didn't know if werewolves did that sort of thing, like it was something only humans would pine for.

She blinked. God, since when had she started thinking of herself as a werewolf? Truth be told, she'd noticed the change creeping up on her this entire past month, ever since she mated with Gage. The pack brothers seemed to like having her around, too, though their trust in Gage still wasn't completely mended. She'd tried her best to be the mediator and help out however she could, but she knew no matter how much she loved Gage and wanted the others to see how much he cared, she couldn't force her pack to like him. A lot of them still resented Gage over what happened with the wraiths.

Gossip within packs was akin to that of a high school. She'd heard stories and whispered talk about their feelings for their Alpha. From what she gathered, she thought they had started to warm up to Gage before the wraith incident, but then shit hit the fan and Gage lost their trust again. It wasn't even his fault they were so distrustful to begin with. Malachite, the witch who'd sent the wraiths after them at that cottage in the woods, and Mistress Black were responsible for the gigantic black hole of mistrust prevalent in the Moonstruck Pack. Danica wished she could rip their throats out for causing so much trouble for her people.

She blinked, startled. Normally, she wasn't one to be so bloodthirsty. That was another aspect about her that had grown this past month with the closer they drew to the full moon and her first official Change.

Unable to resist the pull, she looked toward the window, almost forlorn she'd shut out the beautiful moonlight. In the library back at Crescent Manor, Gage had a collection of old diaries and journals belonging to previous packmasters. Some of them had recorded their first Change. Being a bookworm, Danica had eagerly devoured all the dusty, worn volumes so she'd know what to expect. They all pretty much described the sensation of being a fearless predator as "awesome," but getting to said awesomeness involved a world of pain as the Curse of the Moon literally stretched and morphed every bone and muscle you had. It would hurt like hell the first time. When she'd nervously asked Gage about it, he quickly reassured her that her body would adapt every time she changed, and it would grow easier and eventually be a pleasant experience.

*Yeah. And I bet doctors tell pregnant women the same thing when they go through childbirth.*

A wave of nausea nearly made her puke up her dinner. Holy shit, she was going to turn into a wolf! It sounded crazy even thinking it.

On the verge of hyperventilating, she forced herself to calm down and focus on something else.

Something sexy and with a man-piece she'd like to shower attention on right about now.

Her thoughts drifted back to Gage as the television show ended. He'd been so anxious when he'd left; thanks to their bond, she'd felt his nerves for the duration of his absence. It had been a half hour. The sense of fear and anxiety had only soured while the minutes ticked away, nearly driving her mad. Linked emotions was great when it was all lovey-dovey stuff. With anything negative or angsty, she quickly found herself taking on the mood of her mate, even if she'd been in good spirits previously. Gage had also strained to adjust to the unexplainable mood swings, especially when she'd had her period and he had become overly emotional at a pack meeting. *That* had been entertaining.

Danica leaned her head back against the headboard and sighed. It was so frustrating not being able to tell your own emotions from someone else's. Relationships were hard enough. You'd think knowing how your significant other was feeling all the time would be a good thing, but Danica was starting to feel like she could never get any privacy. Gage promised to teach her to control it and to shut out his emotions, or at least mute them, but even he was struggling with that concept.

Danica smiled wistfully. Despite all the struggle, she knew without a doubt she wouldn't want it any other way. Feeling close to someone, like you're a part of them and they are a part of you, was what she'd always wanted.

Seth leaving her had broken something inside of her, and for a long time she'd been afraid she'd never get it back. She'd been holding on to a thread that not all people were cruel and would abandon her. Seth's abrupt departure, along with his harsh words about her fuller figure and how she was unfit to be seen with him, was the severing blow to that thread of hope. Ever since, she'd kept herself from getting too close to people for fear of them letting her down. It had made for a lonely life, and she thought she could handle it and that she just didn't need any relationships.

Then she met Gage, and it was like seeing the world in color again. The part of her she'd repressed—her ability to feel a connection with someone—had been starving for attention. Mating with Gage had been exactly what she'd needed to feel whole and at peace with herself, her life, and the way things had turned out for her.

Gage's emotions suddenly spiked, his anxiety so palpable it made her breath catch. She sat up, honing in on their connection as his anxiety turned to disbelief, then shock, and then fear.

Her heart beat faster as the swirling emotions all came to a boiling point and spilled over to a darker feeling she hadn't yet sensed through her mate but knew all too well.

*Rage.*

Screw this waiting around crap. She might technically be a queen of wolves, but this wasn't the fifteenth century.

Sometimes men needed rescuing too.

Danica climbed out of bed, slipped on her shoes, and locked up their room. She walked briskly, except when she had to stop once to ask a guard for directions to the assembly room where the meeting was being held.

The closer she drew to her mate, the deeper her frown and brows sank. Something was wrong. Dread crept into her heart as she automatically imagined the worst.

*Nik offended someone, and Gage, being the white knight, intervened and has been horribly wounded. Or maybe someone threatened me and he went totally ape-shit on them and got stripped of his ranking and—shit, shit, shit, Danica! Stop thinking!*

Shouts drifted toward her. She broke into an all-out sprint as she turned the corner, nearly falling flat on her face in the process. She raced toward the crowd gathered in front of the meeting room doors.

Through the tangle of voices, it was hard to hear what was going on. Danica grabbed the nearest bystander, a tall man with dark hair and an expensive-looking suit.

"Hey!" She bit her tongue and cleared her throat. "Excuse me," she said more politely, "but can you tell me what happened?"

The man turned around, his thin upper lip rolled up in disgust. He stared at her hand, which still grasped his arm. Then his gaze rolled up to her face and he grinned. "So glad you could make it in time for the show, my lady."

Danica instantly recoiled, taking a step back. "You're the packmaster of that crazy werewolf who tried to kill me."

His smiled hitched. "*Norman*," he said, over enunciating. "My name is Norman Bl—"

"I remember your name!" she snapped. She looked

past him, too worried about Gage to focus on the creep in front of her. "What happened?"

"Unfortunately, nothing," Norman said, sounding bored. "I so would have liked to have seen Malachite wipe the floor with that insolent pup you call a mate."

As her brain pieced together *mate* and *Malachite* in the same sentence, a spike of terror drove itself straight into Danica's heart. Shoving Norman out of the way, she forced herself to the front of the crowd. Alara stood there, barking orders to her guards to control the crowd and looking all-around harried. Danica couldn't remember ever seeing a hair out of place on her head. She even looked put-together while mating with Nik for crying out loud!

Danica's eyes spotted her mate instantly—as well as the three claw marks marring his cheek.

Her eyes widened. "Gage!" she screamed.

Nik was holding him back, though narrowly. Danica had never seen Gage so angry. His nails were claws and his teeth had morphed into fangs. He was somewhere between beast and man, and it terrified her a little.

But the moment he heard her voice, it was as if all the rage in him vanished. She felt it drain away as he slowly turned and looked at her, his gold eyes returning to that blue hue she so loved to gaze upon.

"Danica," he whispered.

Nik glanced at her and sighed with relief. "Thank God," he said as she approached. "I thought I was going to have to knock him out before he made a further ass of himself."

"What happened?" she said, her voice trembling as

she eyed the angry, puckered skin around the deep lacerations in Gage's face.

Gage and Nik both cast a stony look behind her. "*Him,*" Nik said. "Asshole alert, like, we're talking a Category-Five Prick."

Danica turned toward the wall.

There was no missing the sophisticated yet masculine man who stood there. With his vivid coloring and seven-foot height, he easily stood over most of his fellow werewolves.

The descriptions Gage and Nik had told her all clicked into place, and her voice hardened. "Malachite," she hissed.

The other werewolf blinked, turning his head in her direction. Their eyes locked; he was handsome in a cold, classical way. A bruise bloomed above his eye, which was nearly swollen shut, and Danica smiled inside as she spotted blood welling from his busted lip.

*Way to go, Gage.*

Then Malachite blinked several times, and he went completely pale.

Caught off guard, Danica stared back, unsure what to do. Why was he looking at her like that, as if he'd seen a ghost?

She watched his lips form the words, "Oh my God," before he strode toward her.

Nik and Gage instantly shielded her, both men growling and snarling as their former Alpha approached. Malachite never took his eyes off her, and it made her want to shrink away and hide behind her mate.

But she wasn't the type of girl who could hide anymore.

She wouldn't, couldn't. Hiding implied weakness, and she couldn't afford for her or Gage to be seen as vulnerable.

*A king is not weak. Neither is a queen. As Gage has said before, appearances mean everything in this world.*

Inserting her arms in the space between Nik and Gage, she stepped between them and straightened her spine. She stared up into Malachite's gaze defiantly. "Yeah? What's your problem?"

Malachite didn't speak. His mouth was open in shock as he searched her face so minutely she thought he might be trying to memorize it.

Growling, she snapped her fingers in front of his face. "Hello? Did you not hear me?"

He blinked and roughly cleared his throat, shaking his head and hiding his gaze as his long hair fell over his shoulders. "Forgive me, my lady," he said in a velvety soft voice. "I was just wondering if I was imagining things again."

*Huh?*

"What are you talking about?" Danica demanded. "Where the hell do you get off attacking my mate?"

Malachite's head jerked up and Danica froze. There was so much pain in his eyes, like the man's heart held a thousand sorrows.

Stunned, she couldn't help but stare at him. He looked so… tortured. Based on the stories she'd heard, she'd almost expected him to show up in a cape while twirling his token villainous mustache.

Malachite's expression twisted in anguish. "Tell me it's not true." Danica tensed as he reached up and gently cupped her cheek. "You can't be mated. You're supposed to—"

"Get the hell off her!" Gage roared, knocking away Malachite's hand and pulling her against his chest. He pointed a finger at the other werewolf. "Don't you dare touch her again."

Tucking Danica into his side, he turned them away and started forcing a path through the crowd.

Guards started after them. "Hey! Halt right this instant!"

"Let them go!" Alara ordered. Her guards didn't look too pleased, but they obeyed all the same.

Nik hurriedly walked beside them, glancing between Alara and Gage.

"Don't worry," Danica said. "I've got him."

Nik glanced at his brother one more time with worry, then curtly nodded before joining Alara.

As they broke free of the crowd and Danica started to turn back around, her eyes again roved over the man who had brought her beloved so much pain.

A man who still stared at her as if he couldn't bear to look away.

# CHAPTER FOUR

DANICA TRIED TO WATCH WHERE SHE WAS GOING BUT found it nearly impossible to take her eyes off her mate. Though the claw marks on his face were healing rapidly, the sight of the angry lacerations filled her with rage. She was tempted to turn around and claw Malachite's eyes out, but a larger part of her wanted nothing more than to put as much distance between him and her mate as possible.

Neither she nor Gage said a word on the way back to their room. Nobody bothered them, but plenty of people stared. Danica practiced her "royal-slash-I-don't-give-a-shit" look by keeping her chin lifted and pretending not to see them. There would be more than enough gossip to go around without fueling the fire.

The second they entered their room, Danica locked the door and immediately pulled Gage into the bathroom. She knew baths helped him relax. They'd often enjoyed long bubble baths together back at Crescent Manor.

"Shirt. Off," she commanded, grabbing a washcloth and turning on the hot water in the large tub. Steam wafted off the water as she dumped in a dollop of bubble bath.

*Rip!*

Danica whirled and her brows rose. "What are you—?"

She didn't have time to finish the sentence because Gage, his muscular, sweaty chest now bared, closed the distance between them in two purposeful strides and crushed his mouth to hers.

She blinked in surprise, not having time to prepare as his tongue pried her lips open and slipped inside her mouth. She moaned as he cupped her sex through the fabric of her silk dress, rubbing his fingers along her seam.

"Gage," she finally gasped. "What are you doing?"

"I need you," he said roughly, almost growling it. "Now." He seized the back of her head and pulled her mouth onto his again in another hungry kiss. She could feel her control slipping away as something inside her, something more feral, whimpered to be set free. As her brain tried to process what was happening, her hands eagerly sought out his zipper. He groaned as she pulled it down and yanked his pants toward the floor. He stepped out of them, kicking them aside as she pulled at his boxers.

No matter how many times they made love—which was often—she could never get enough of him.

His swollen cock jutted outward, only an inch from her face. She was about to stand when her carnal instincts took over, and she took him into her mouth.

He groaned as she sucked him, rolling her tongue over the head of his cock. His hips bucked as she worked.

"God, yes, Danica. Just like that."

Fire grew beneath her belly, making her ache with need. Releasing him, she stood as he growled in protest. Grinning mischievously, she placed a finger to his lips, hushing him. She leaned forward until her lips were next to his ear. "You know what feels better than my mouth?" she said, nipping at his earlobe. She grabbed his hand and slid it up her skirt to the slickness begging to be touched.

That was all it took. Any last ounce of control Gage had went out the door as he seized the neckline of her dress and tore it clean down the middle. Throwing the scraps of ruined silk to the floor, he tore at her bra next. Her breasts sprang free, and he caught a puckered nipple in his mouth, teasing and sucking on it.

She whimpered, pressing her chest against him as his other hand pulled at her soaked panties. She could barely think as she stepped out of them, nearly tripping herself in the process as he picked her up and sat them in the tub. She had just enough sense to reach behind her and turn off the faucet before Gage planted her on his cock and began moving his hips.

She spread her thighs as far as she could to take his extra girth in, moaning as his shaft pierced her sweet spot over and over in slow, sensual movements. He drove deep within her, filling her up in a grinding rhythm that set her blood ablaze. Sweat broke out along her brow, and she knew it had nothing to do with the bath temperature. The steamy water sloshed around them, bubbles soaking their skin as he kneaded her breasts and kissed the cherry nubs of her nipples. "I'll never get tired of these," he murmured, sounding out of breath. "They're so perfect. I can barely get a handful." He cupped a breast in each palm and squeezed in rhythm to his strokes.

She cried out, grinding her hips and her sex harder against him. "Oh, Gage."

"Yes," he said, working her harder. "Come for me."

He didn't have to say it twice. Pleasure exploded in her, and she cried out as she writhed against him, trying to draw out the orgasm for as long as possible.

She felt his hot seed pour into her a moment later as he groaned deep in his throat, thrusting a few more times before slowing and stopping altogether.

They sat like that for a minute, both panting as she laid against his chest. She loved listening to his heartbeat and the feeling of closeness it brought. His heart was racing nearly as fast as her own. She stared at his tattoos, the patterns of which were identical to the ones marking her skin. Seeing them brought a smile to her face every time, reminding her she was his and he was hers, and that neither of them was ever truly alone.

He idly twirled a damp strand of her hair around his finger. "I'm sorry," he murmured.

She looked up at her mate. "For what?"

"For pouncing on you like that," he admitted with a boyish grin that she adored. "The fight brought my wolf to the surface, and I guess I hadn't quite tamed it before you brought me in here and demanded I strip down."

"It's okay," she said with a smile, leaning forward and kissing him. "My inner wolf was restless too."

"You can feel it?" he asked with an excited sparkle in

his eyes.

She nodded. "All I can think about is being outside. Or on top of you," she admitted sheepishly.

He laughed, and the hearty sound rumbled through her chest. "It's only going to get worse the closer we get to midnight. Come on. Let's wash up and get ready to go."

He turned her around so his legs were on either side of her and tucked her against him as he grabbed a cloth and began washing her back. It was so sweet she couldn't help but snuggle up against him. She almost hated to sour the moment, but she had to ask. "So that was Malachite, huh?"

The washcloth paused in its trek across her shoulder blades. "Yes," Gage said darkly, continuing to wash her.

"Is he here to put his name in for king?"

"I don't know why he's here," Gage sighed. "He isn't an Alpha and he isn't mated, so he can't be king."

"Hmmm…." Danica worried her lip. "Why do you think he acted that way around me? It was like he'd seen a ghost."

"I don't know. He was always off-kilter." Gage growled, pulling her into him and wrapping his thickly muscled arms around her. "But I swear I won't let him harm you."

She rested her head against his chest and closed her eyes, savoring the quiet moment.

*And I swear not to ever let him hurt you again.*

She could feel his protective urges toward her, as well as the dark, undeniable truth he would kill for her.

Could she ever kill someone? She had never considered it to be in her nature to take a life, but she knew all the same she'd do whatever it took to protect Gage.

The conversation shifted to other things—werewolf politics, mostly—and the mood was noticeably more somber. As they dried off and got dressed quietly, both of them lost in their own thoughts, Danica couldn't help but fear this might be as good as it gets in this world.

A stolen moment here and there, never knowing when your next kiss might be your last….

She'd always wanted an exciting life, but now that she had one, she found that "boring" sounded a lot more appetizing.

*The grass is always greener….*

A frantic knock at the door startled them. Gage glanced at her. "Wait here." He went to the door. She could hear Nik speaking in hushed tones on the other side.

Danica padded closer.

"Are you sure?" Gage said. "She's probably lying in an attempt to get closer to Danica. What if she's an assassin?"

"Alara doesn't seem to think so. She had one of her best witches scan her with a lie detector spell."

"Oh, right, so I suppose since your mate says it's okay, it's fine to put mine in harm's way."

"Easy," Nik growled.

Gage sighed. "Sorry. My mouth ran away with me. I'm just… fried."

He lowered his voice, as did Nik. Danica had a hard time hearing what they were saying, but Gage didn't look happy. He pressed his lips together, deep in thought. She could hear Nik arguing with him. Finally, Gage nodded. "Very well. I'll meet with her."

He shut the door and hurriedly finished buttoning up his shirt.

"What was that all about?" Danica asked.

"Nothing important."

She crossed her arms and cocked her hip. "Really? That's the best line you can give me?"

He stopped and slowly grinned. "I gotta be more careful around you, or you're going to learn to read me like a book."

"Already can, love," she said with a smile as he came over and kissed her.

Worry creased his brows. "Look, Nik says there's a witch here to see us."

"And?"

"…It's the same witch who owns the cabin in the woods."

She stared. "With the crazy wraiths?"

Gage nodded.

"*Oh*. Wow. What does she want?"

"She says she has information that's valuable to us, but she'll only speak to me—and you."

Danica weighed the decision. "It could make or break our victory in this war against the witches. I say we go." She started for the door when he grabbed her wrist and stopped her.

"It could be a mistake. What if this is a trap?"

"So what if it is? What if staying here and refusing to see her is the greater mistake?"

The frown he gave her said he didn't like this decision one bit, but as a leader, she knew he couldn't fault her logic.

They were really no better off than they were in regards to finding out Mistress Black's true motives. If seeing this mystery witch could somehow help the Underworld....

"Very well. We'll go," he said at last.

She laced her fingers with his and squeezed his hand.

"We'll go together."

# CHAPTER FIVE

GAGE COULDN'T HELP BUT THINK "THIS IS A BAD IDEA" the entire time he, Danica, and Nik walked to the room where the witch informant was waiting.

Nik had advised them both not to make a sound, thus the silence had stretched so taut that Gage thought his nerves would snap altogether.

This part of the palace was infrequently used. Though everything still shone with fresh polish, it became clear from the tomb-like silence enveloping them that the only visitors in this wing were palace staff and the occasional patrol.

Nik paused by a wall, glanced in either direction, and lifted up the flap of a tapestry to reveal a door. It nearly blended in with the stone walls; someone was a remarkable artist. The tapestry's surface had been painted in the same shades of blue and gray to match the texture of the stone around it.

A cool draft smelling of damp earth greeted them as they followed Nik inside the hidden tunnel. A flashlight beam split the darkness, lighting the narrow, winding staircase as they went deeper into the earth.

"Hardly anyone knows about this passage," Nik said quietly. "Alara said back during the wars, the royal family kept their prisoners down here."

"Charming," Gage said dryly. In a way he found it fascinating. The inner architectural geek in him wanted to explore the old parts of the castle, but his enthusiasm would have to wait. Now, he needed information. He needed to find out why this woman who had cost him so much had suddenly decided to seek him out and supposedly help him.

The stairwell ended in a long corridor with no lights. Rusting prison bars shone in the sterile light of the flashlight.

Danica clung to his hand, her nails biting into his skin. "They don't still keep people down here, do they?" she asked with a quaver in her voice, staring warily at the darkness within each cell as they passed.

Nik grinned at her. "Nope. But wouldn't it make a kinky place to mate? Each cell already comes equipped with shackles and a cot."

"Nik…" Gage warned.

"All right, all right. Just saying."

Gage shook his head. He was hoping Nik's more carnal tendencies would settle down once he'd mated, but he could see that wasn't likely to happen anytime soon.

Once past the dungeons, Nik led them to a small room

with sparse candlelight. It might have been romantic, had shackles and an Iron Maiden not been in the corner of the room.

The hairs on the back of Gage's neck stood on end, and he raised a brow. "We're meeting the informant in a torture chamber? Really?"

Nik shrugged. "This place gives what few people know about it the creeps. Naturally, they try to avoid it. Alara thought it to be the least likely place you'd be discovered."

Danica looked around her with a morbid sense of curiosity. "I can't imagine why this place would freak anybody out. It's so homey."

Gage snorted.

Nik whipped out his phone and texted someone. A moment later, the door opened and four figures stepped inside.

Alara lowered the hood of her cloak, her brown curls tumbling out over her shoulders. Two guards flanked her, perfectly stone-faced.

Nik went to his mate and gave her a surprisingly tender kiss on the cheek. "You all right?"

Alara nodded. "I'm fine." She glanced at Danica and Gage. "You ready?"

Gage glanced at Danica, who nodded with a firm squeeze to his hand. He looked back at Alara. "Ready as I'll ever be. Let's hear this groundbreaking testimony."

Alara nodded and stepped aside, motioning someone forward. A smaller, robed figure hesitantly stepped into the room, and two frail hands lowered the hood that cloaked her face in shadow.

Gage blinked. Judging from the state of the cabin in the woods, he'd been expecting more of a fairy tale witch, complete with brittle white hair, warts, and a snaggle-toothed leer.

What he received instead was a beautiful, pale woman with flowing light-blonde hair and big violet eyes with sooty lashes.

Danica shifted her weight. Gage squeezed her hand to let her know he wasn't the least bit interested in the woman and that he was merely surprised.

"This is Violet," Alara said. "Violet, this is—"

"I know who they are," she said with a soft voice bearing quiet strength. Suddenly, she fell to her knees and bowed low. Words poured from her mouth. "Please forgive me. Oh God, I didn't have a choice. She said if I didn't do as she asked, she'd kill my family—"

"Whoa, whoa." Gage knelt and reached for her. The second his fingers brushed her shoulder, she flinched like a dog expecting to be beaten. Glancing at Danica in puzzlement, he withdrew his hand but remained kneeling before her. "I'm not going to hurt you."

The woman trembled. "But you want to," she whispered. "Anyone would want to after what I did."

Gage's hand tightened into a fist as anger surged through him. Violet was right. Oh, how he wanted to hurt her. He swore he'd never strike a woman, but he was sorely tempted to make an exception. He wanted to kill her, to cause her as much pain as she had caused him. "You were coerced?"

She nodded, still trembling.

He sat there, unsure what to do. Comforting women had never been his strong suit.

Luckily, Danica was an expert. Her nurturing instincts must have kicked in because she knelt beside him. "It's okay," she said gently. "You don't have to be afraid. We're not going to hurt you."

Something in Danica's voice soothed Violet's tremors. She slowly looked up with those wide, violet eyes that were no doubt her namesake, and stared at Danica. Tears brimmed along the rims of her eyes and fell in silent streams down her pale cheeks. "You're more beautiful in person," she said, reaching out to touch a strand of Danica's hair.

Gage instantly grabbed Danica and pulled her up with him, keeping her out of reach of Violet.

Violet let her hand drop and ducked her head in shame. "I deserve that. I can't blame you for not trusting me."

"That's an understatement," Nik muttered under his breath.

Alara elbowed him and gave him a stern look, then gazed at Violet. "Why don't you start at the beginning? How did you get involved with Mistress Black?"

Violet blinked away her tears, her child-like face becoming more businesslike as she nodded. "Of course," she murmured, standing. She clutched at her cloak as if to drive away a chill while her eyes grew distant. "I've always tried to stay away from witch politics, but the scope and depth of my powers have often forced me into the spotlight. Despite my best efforts at hiding myself away and pretending to be a nutcase, I attracted the attention of some powerful people." She gulped. "When I wouldn't comply with their demands, they forced my hand by kidnapping my family and threatening to kill them should I not cooperate." Her tears started falling all over again. "Please understand. I didn't have a choice! If there were any other options, I would have taken them. I even tried killing myself to stop the Order, but they kept watch over me day and night to ensure I did myself no harm before my job was done." Her face grew more haunted. "And even after I finished the deed, they didn't let me go."

"Is that how you met Onyx? Through the Order?" Gage asked.

Violet nodded, looking miserable. "I'm the one who sold the spell to him."

"We know," Nik said sourly. "We found that out the day we met your wraiths. Charming, they were, especially as they were ripping our comrades to pieces."

"Nik," Alara snapped.

"It's okay," Violet said, crying uncontrollably now. "It's the truth. They made me cast that spell before taking me prisoner."

"How did you escape?" Gage asked.

"I didn't—but my astral form did."

Everyone's brows rose but Danica's. "What?" she said, looking around. "What am I missing? Is that a big deal or something?"

"Only the most powerful witches and warlocks can project themselves outside their bodies," Gage said, staring at Violet. She looked so real. To be able to put that amount of detail into the spell....

He shivered at the power this young woman wielded. No wonder she'd been so attractive to her captors. He almost felt sorry for her because he knew that power was more of a curse than a gift.

"There's more," Violet said. "As if you don't hate me enough," she muttered miserably.

Gage wasn't sure he could hate her any more than he already did, but he remained silent. Though brutally honest at times, he was not cruel. "Go on."

Violet stood there, gathering her thoughts. Her throat flashed as she swallowed hard and inhaled a deep breath. "The High King was the one who placed the hit on Danica's head."

"Tell us something we don't know," Nik drawled, only to earn another reprimanding glare from Alara.

Violet shook her head. "What you don't know is that he paid for a reading in order to find out if he'd ever be toppled from his throne." She met Gage's gaze. "He knew you would be his greatest threat, but he also knew that in order for you to overtake him, you'd have to be mated."

Gage went still. "What are you saying?"

Violet seemed to brace herself as the room held its breath.

"I'm saying I'm the one who sold him the premonition that resulted in him putting a hit on your mate's head."

Gage stood there, dumbfounded.

Then his control snapped.

He lunged for Violet, claws aimed at her throat, when Nik and the two guards intervened.

"You bitch!" Gage spat. "I'll kill you for this!"

"Brother!" Nik yelled, struggling to contain Gage, who'd halfway transformed into a wolf. "Calm down!"

Danica ran forward, grabbing hold of Gage's face and forcing him to look at her. "Gage, look at me."

His eyes stared into hers, and he started to calm down.

"I need you to hold it together," she said firmly. "Yes, what she did was wrong on so many levels, but she risked coming here tonight to tell us the truth about what happened so we may be able to stop the enemy. Isn't that what we wanted? Wasn't that the whole point to this? Killing our only informant won't do us any good, and you know damn well she's the best lead we've had."

Gage blinked and the wolf in him vanished. Nik and the guards slowly stepped away, though they lingered beside him should he snap again.

He ran his hands through his hair and over his face. God, he felt so ragged. How much more shit would he have to put up with before he could finally find peace with his mate? Why couldn't the world just leave them alone? "I'm sorry," he said wearily. "I couldn't help it. Today's been hard on me."

Danica pressed her lips together. Gage knew she was thinking about the source of his anxiety—about Malachite—and he appreciated the fact she had enough sensitivity to not speak his enemy's name aloud right now and put him even more on edge.

Violet trembled from her spot beside Alara.

Gage turned to her and gave her his best apologetic smile. "I'm sorry. I promise it won't happen again."

Violet searched his eyes before at last nodding.

A moment passed as the tension in the room subsided somewhat before Gage spoke again. His voice was ragged from the aftereffects of partially changing so many times today. "The High King belonged to the Order of the Sun. Do you know what they want?"

A shadow passed over Violet's eyes as her skin paled. "To bring about the Cleansing, which Mistress Black believes she can instigate."

"Cleansing? That sounds like some apocalyptic shit," Nik said.

Violet began to ramble, as if driven by her fear. "She means to rid the world of those she believes to be inferior to her, both human and paranormal alike. She surrounds herself with powerful paranormals, not just in magical ability, but people who hold significant political sway. She's everywhere, always watching. Not even the DPI is resistant."

Gage looked at Nik, who frowned. Did Verika know the DPI was compromised? They'd have to figure out a way to reach her later without drawing attention to the fact they now knew there was a mole. Now that Violet had come forward, they couldn't risk leaking any information that would lead back to her. Danica was right—Violet was the best lead they had.

Maybe the only one they'd get. They had to play this carefully and correctly.

Alara stepped forward. "Do you think you could find out more?"

Violet shivered, shaking her head. "I don't think

spying—"

"What if we offered you protection?" Alara said, interrupting her. There was a hunger in her eyes, a spark that thirsted for blood. Gage could understand it after what had happened to her. The Order had cost Alara her entire family. Gage would want revenge too. If Nik had noticed the subtle change in Alara's normally docile demeanor, he hadn't mentioned it to him.

Violet shuddered and looked away. "None of you can protect me. I'm already as good as dead."

"Do you know where you are?" Gage asked.

Violet shook her head. "They keep me blindfolded when moving me in and out. I know it's a city because I can hear the cars honking at all hours, but I could not tell you where."

*Great. A city. That's helpful.*

Alara grasped Violet's hands. "If you deliver us more information, I swear to you you'll be granted amnesty once we defeat Mistress Black and shut down the mafia."

"What?" Gage said, anger making his voice sharp. "After everything she's done?"

"She's trying to help us!" Alara snapped, whirling on him. "The DPI is all but useless, and this is the only whiff of the mafia we've had since my family's murder. And I will be damned if I'm letting a chance at justice slip through my fingers that easily."

They all stared at her. Nik rested a hand on her shoulder. "Alara—"

"Don't, Nik," she said, shrugging him off and returning her attention to Violet. "Well? Will you consider?"

Violet looked around at them. "You swear you'll protect me?"

"On my life," Alara said without hesitation. "As will they," she added pointedly, throwing everyone a look over her shoulder.

Gage growled low in his throat, but Danica calmed him by placing a hand on his forearm.

*Alara's right*, Danica said in his head. *We have no other connections to Mistress Black, and we don't know if another opportunity like this will appear.*

Gage silently swore. His mate was right, as usual. While he could see the sense in her reasoning, he also couldn't help but loathe the creature standing in front of him.

The woman who'd nearly cost him everything.

And not only that, but how could he hope to protect her, a captive of the most wicked witch they'd encountered, when he didn't even know if he could protect his mate or his pack? No matter how much he wanted her to pay for her sins, he knew they needed an insider. As much as he hated to admit it, Violet could be the key to saving them all. The chance was too sweet to pass up.

"Fine," Gage barked. "But I want you to understand something. The moment you become a liability to her"—he gestured at Danica—"is the moment I stop protecting you."

Violet's eyes flickered to Danica. Her face never once betrayed any hurt she might have felt at Gage's harsh words. Her lips twitched up into the barest whisper of a smile. "As I said, I'm already dead anyway, but the thought of you trying to save me is nice. It makes me feel not so alone in this."

Gage winced, almost feeling guilty.

"I can't fault you on trying to protect the ones you love," Violet said. Her expression turned serious as she looked at Alara, who awaited an answer. "I swear to you I'll do everything in my power to help. Should you need to reach me—" she reached into the folds of her cloak and produced a shiny glass disc, which she handed to Alara— "break this and I'll come to you if I can. But choose wisely when to use it because you can only use it once."

She whirled. Her eyes frantically searched for a sound the others did not hear. "I must go. They're coming."

With that, her image flickered out of existence, like a television screen fading away after being shut off.

Nik sighed hard. "That went well."

"At least we have a lead now," Alara said, staring at the disc in her hand. "Violet's given us more hope than I could have imagined."

"And more heartache," Gage said darkly.

Alara gave him a brief, sympathetic glance before her face hardened once more. "I'm sorry. I understand your plight, but at the same time, I cannot allow a chance like this to slip through my fingers. I have my people to think of."

He couldn't fault her for that. It was the Alpha's curse, a burden you took on whenever you assumed the role of shepherd—the good of the people came before your own personal feelings.

That principle alone made him feel a little dirty. He'd

promised Violet safety, but if the time called for it, he'd abandon her to the wolves if it meant protecting Danica. Since when had he compromised his values?

*From the moment you met your soul mate.*

He glanced at Danica, feeling an overwhelming surge of love and protectiveness. Yes, by mating with her he'd become more vulnerable, but at the same time, her love and devotion gave him strength. For that alone, he could not resent her.

The others spoke quietly while he thought to himself. Danica touched his arm. "You okay?"

"Yeah," Gage said at last. "Just thinking about that girl. And about what I said."

Danica sighed hard. "It had to be done. It seems like everything at this level of politics is 'an eye for an eye.'"

She was right. All his life, Gage had fought to be fair and just, and that just wouldn't cut it anymore. He knew deep in his heart that in order to win this war, he couldn't play the game the same way he used to. The ante had been upped, and he couldn't afford to lose, even if it meant sacrificing a pawn.

He couldn't be "perfect Gage" anymore.

"You think we can trust her?" Danica asked him.

"It looks like we won't have a choice," Gage muttered, shooting Alara a contemplative look. Ever since the funeral, something had shifted in his brother's mate.

The innocent young woman who might have been there before was now gone, replaced by a darker and more dangerous version. Gage understood that darkness, the biting, scratching urge to seek revenge. He just hoped Nik could help her tame the inner beast before it consumed what light was left in her soul.

Thinking about everything going on right now, Gage felt the pressure of his world closing in on him. If he didn't fight back, he'd be crushed by his own circumstances, and he knew there were plenty of enemies who would love to see him fall.

He would not let that happen. It wasn't just a pride thing. It was the principle of the matter.

He was done running. He was ready to take a stand and protect the ones he loved.

And in order to do that, he was going to need more power.

A weird sense of rightness pulled at his gut, like this outcome had been inevitable from the start. It made it somewhat easier to accept what he had to do.

"Alara," he said, stopping their group as they began to file out of the room.

She turned, raising a brow. "Yes?"

Gage's jaw ticked as he finally made a decision that would ultimately change his life.

"I've changed my mind. I'm running for High King."

# CHAPTER SIX

MALACHITE WIPED THE LAST OF THE BLOOD FROM HIS face and wrung the washcloth under the water. Red streams floated down the drain, staining the water pink. He ran a hand over his face and examined his skin in the bathroom mirror of his private suite. Already the cut along his jawline had healed, though Gage's right hook had made it hard to chew without shooting needle-like pain into the roots of his teeth and down his neck.

A sense of pride welled up in Malachite, briefly cutting through his irritation. The pup's older brother might have taught him how to throw a punch, but it was Malachite who'd taught him to fight dirty. And judging from the way he'd tackled him in the hallway, a little bit of Malachite's teachings remained embedded in his bones. Malachite smiled.

*I told you, Gage. No matter how hard you try, you will never truly be rid of me.*

Feeling satisfied, Malachite turned off the bathroom light and walked into his bedroom. The furnishings were exactly to his taste, reflective of the old-world elegance he so favored. Growing up in the 1700s had made him adverse to modern designs. They were so bland and tasteless. Where was the personality in a machine-manufactured piece of furniture? How could a machine love a work of art?

A familiar itch made him clench and unclench his fist. Going over to his suitcase, he removed a small leather bag and took out a block of cedar and a carving knife. Among the knife's other more entertaining uses—like carving up the flesh of those who'd been foolish enough to piss him off—Malachite found solace in whittling. The pastime was methodical, the act of stroking and chipping away at the wood and pouring all his focus into it. When he was creating, he didn't have to think or remember his past. And that in itself was a great mercy to his troubled soul.

Almost unbidden, Danica's face flashed before his eyes, and he cut himself. He stared at the blood welling from the cut, which had almost instantly begun to seal.

Seeing Danica had been like a punch to the gut that had knocked the wind completely out of him. Nothing could have prepared him for how closely she resembled his dead Emily.

Images from his violent past drifted to the forefront of his mind, a grim slideshow he could never seem to completely forget: coming home from a hard day's work to find his wife and child slaughtered by a rogue pack of werewolves, the wooden floors of his house slick with their freshly spilled blood, the feeling of the earth dropping out from under him as it struck him what had happened. It was the same day he'd discovered his capacity for killing in cold blood as a rage he'd never known overtook him.

He closed his eyes, seeing his wife's terrified green eyes staring up at him as he held her, her cheek and throat marred by the deep claw marks that had severed her artery. Sorrow washed over him as the faces of his beautiful wife and child filled his head. Their laughter and screams mingled in his thoughts, racing faster and faster, until he couldn't stand it anymore.

Rising, he roared and hurled the knife across the room. It embedded in the wood beside the door, the zing of the metal ringing as it vibrated within the ivory handle.

Staggering toward the mini-fridge, he grabbed a tankard of whiskey and knocked the bottle straight back. Large gulps of the stout amber liquid burned his throat, but he didn't care. He welcomed the pain, to feel anything else other than the sorrow of losing his family.

Some days were better than others. He could almost forget about his Emily and the infant son he'd never get to know if he went several days purposefully not thinking of them, which was next to impossible. He was always thinking of them in the back of his mind, just as he had when they were alive. God, if he'd known love could hurt this badly, he never would have sought it out to start with.

It was the only thing holding him back now from taking Danica as his own. She was still young, as his Emily had been when they wed. What if Danica too was torn from him? Could he survive that kind of agony again?

Was there enough of the man he used to be left to love her the way she needed to be loved?

Despite his fears, the urge to see her was like a drug. Seeing her standing there and staring at him in the hallway had been like a slap to the face. There she was, a woman he never thought he'd see again, come back to him. She even smelled the same as his Emily, like wildflowers and sunshine.

He yearned to bury his hands in her hair, to taste her sweetness as he had on their wedding night.

He glanced at the half-downed tankard, then at the door. She was probably in her room right now. With her scent still fresh in his nostrils, it wouldn't be hard to track her down. *How much of a fool are you, Malachite?*

The promise of happiness was too great to ignore. Grabbing his coat, he started for the hall with the full intent of seeking out Danica.

He opened the door and paused.

Norman stood there with his fist raised as if he'd been about to knock. He blinked in surprise. "I'm sorry, were you heading out?"

Malachite glared at Norman. "What do you want?"

The older wolf raised both hands. "I come in peace, I assure you."

"Just as you did for Danica, I hear."

Norman rolled his eyes. "For the last time, I didn't know anything about Onyx's business interactions. Otherwise, I would have intervened. Now if you'll please let me in, I have a proposition I think you'll be most interested in hearing."

"What could you possibly have to offer me that I can't obtain myself?"

Norman's calculating eyes glittered. "A mate."

Malachite's heart stuttered. Maybe it did know how to work after all. "I lost my mate."

"You lost a wife," Norman corrected. "As she was human when she died, the mating curse does not apply to you."

Malachite growled. "She was my wife. In human terms, that makes her my mate."

"Fine, fine," Norman said dismissively, waving a hand as if this were a trivial detail. "She was your mate. Do you want to hear what I have to say or not?"

"What makes you think I'm interested in taking a mate?" Malachite said, crossing his arms.

Norman smiled. "The way you looked at Danica Johnson this evening."

Malachite stared at Norman, unsure what he was getting at.

Norman leaned forward and lowered his voice. "What would you say if I told you that you could claim her for your own?"

Malachite snorted. "I'd tell you you're high on something. Everyone knows you can't break the mating spell."

"Ah, but as we all know, every spell has a loophole. It's just a matter of finding it."

"…And I suppose you're here to tell me you've found it."

"Precisely."

Malachite studied him. The Nightshade Pack was

infamous for its inability to be trusted, except when it came to eventually stabbing all of their allies in the back and changing allegiances at the last minute.

"Not interested," Malachite said, starting to shut the door.

"You're lying," Norman hissed, sticking his foot in the door to keep it from shutting. "I see the way you looked at Danica. Just imagine my surprise. The mighty Malachite, tamed by a pup."

Malachite's gums ached as his teeth elongated into fangs. "Come a little closer and I'll show you tame."

Norman chuckled. "I admire your ruthlessness. It's an underappreciated trait we both share."

"Get out," Malachite snapped.

"Hear me out, and I'll be on my way."

Norman stared at him, making it clear he wasn't moving anytime soon. He was so lithe, Malachite could probably throw him through the wall, but he'd already caused enough of a stir earlier. If he outright harmed an Alpha, he'd be thrown out of the castle for sure. Which would defeat the whole purpose of him coming....

When he first saw Danica's picture in a werewolf magazine, all he could think of was, *There's my Emily, come back to me.* When he heard of the werewolf summit and how all the royals were invited, he knew he had to attend. He hadn't counted on all of the ensuing drama with the witch mafia and the murder of the High King, but it was of no consequence to him.

All he wanted was Danica. What had started out as mere curiosity soon turned into full-blown obsession once he'd seen her.

He had to have her, no matter what.

The overwhelming desire to be reunited with his lost love, Emily, overtook him.

Reluctantly, he stepped aside.

"That's a good lad," Norman said, coming in and making himself at home in a chair.

Malachite shut the door and turned.

Norman raised his brows. "Won't you sit?"

"I prefer to stand, thanks."

"Touchy." Norman *tsk-tsked*.

"Get on with it. What the hell do you have to offer?"

Norman's smile hitched. "Very well," he said more tightly than he had before. "What do you know of the mating spell?"

Malachite nearly rolled his eyes. "It's absolute and can only be broken when one mate dies."

"But what if one mate doesn't have to die? What if the spell can be broken?"

Malachite barked a laugh. "That's not possible."

"What if I told you I could deliver the woman you want most into the palm of your hand?"

Malachite paused. "I'd tell you that you were full of shit."

Norman laughed. "Possibly. It wouldn't be the first time I'd heard that."

"I'm not killing Gage, if that's what you want," Malachite said firmly. No way was he going to hurt Danica like that. He'd heard the pain of losing a mate was almost unbearable since the two werewolves were psychically linked. It would be like ripping out a part of your soul. Though he had attained his Alpha rank in Moonstruck by killing the former Alpha in an unfair duel and terrorizing his pack into submission, despite not yet claiming a mate for himself, he knew from personal experience how painful it was to lose someone you love.

"Who said anything about killing?" Norman said innocently. "All we would need to break the link would be a tiny blood sample from each werewolf and poof! No more mating bond."

"Then Black Magic is involved."

"Possibly." Norman's eyes glittered.

Malachite shook his head. "Black Magic is too unpredictable. Besides, losing a mate is supposed to have dire consequences on the wolf left alive. Like never being able to feel love or emotion again, or trying to commit suicide from the sudden emptiness of the psychic bond being snapped."

"All side effects my witch can remedy, I assure you," Norman said with a careless wave of his hand.

"And you know of a witch powerful enough to do this?" Malachite said dryly.

"Yes."

Malachite stared at him suspiciously. "What's in it for you?"

Norman slowly smiled. "You mean, what's in it for *us*? We both share a mutual dislike of a certain Alpha. Taking his mate from him will break him so irreparably, he'll be removed from the picture altogether."

The pieces fell together. "And an unmated Alpha

cannot run for High King."

"Exactly," Norman purred.

Malachite smirked. "You feel that threatened by him that you'd resort to dealing with the forbidden arts just to see him ruined?"

"He is inexperienced in the ways of our world," Norman snapped, his eyes hardening. "This nation needs someone with backbone and experience to take it to the next level."

"The next level being…?"

"Acceptance."

Malachite rolled his eyes. "That's right. I forgot you're a radical. No matter how romantic a notion, humans will never accept us into society. We'd be labeled a danger, a menace. We'd be captured and dissected. We'd have millions more enemies to worry about, considering humans outnumber us a thousand to one."

"Which is exactly why we'll need someone strong enough to do what it takes to get us to a safe place where we can successfully merge with the human race. I know for a fact I'm not the only one tired of hiding." When Malachite made no response, Norman added, "I could give you a place among my court."

"I'm not interested in power," Malachite said without hesitation. His leadership role had nearly gotten him killed the last time. He had no desire to relive that experience again.

Norman studied him. "You have not aligned yourself with a different pack since being dethroned. Being a rogue must get lonely. Surely you'll want a mate then if you do not want power."

Malachite's eyes hardened. "I'll think about it."

Norman's jaw ticked. Rising, he reached into his jacket pocket and pulled out an engraved gold box full of business cards. "Well, I can see you're going to need some time to digest this. Should you change your mind, you know where to find me."

He started to leave and paused by the door. "Oh, and, Malachite, do try to decide soon. This offer is time-sensitive."

With his warning still hanging in the air, he sauntered out the door and closed it behind him.

Malachite stared at the card.

Could it really be possible to make Danica his? She was practically his Emily come back to life. It had to be a sign.

Finally, his loneliness was coming to an end.

But this wasn't something he could fully embrace yet. He knew better than anyone that every bargain had a price.

The question was, was he willing to pay it? At one point, he and Gage had been pack brothers. Those ties were closer than family.

Could he commit the ultimate betrayal of pack blood and stab Gage Johnson in the back?

# CHAPTER SEVEN

AFTER THE DUNGEON ESCAPADE, NIK AND ALARA HAD bidden Gage and Danica farewell so they could prepare for her first Change. She and Gage made a quick trip to their room for some supplies, then they headed outside toward the woods.

Danica's breath caught as the moonlight spilled across her skin, making it tingle like mad. It felt like a thousand tiny bubbles were popping all along her body. It tickled, which made her giggle.

Gage walked beside her, carrying the duffel bag of necessities on his shoulder. He smiled. "Isn't it incredible?"

"Yes," she breathed, reaching out with her other senses. She could feel the pulse of the earth in her bones, could feel every blade of grass and hear every beat of delicate insect wings. "It's like I'm connected to nature in a way I've never been before, like the woods are calling me home."

He took her hand and pulled her forward. "It gets

better once you're a wolf." He winced. "Though getting to that point won't be a picnic."

She nodded, and they kept walking down the gravel drive and into the meadow surrounding the castle. Her mind warred with her body's urge to change as the logical part of her clung to her humanity. Her heart—her soul—longed to be free.

Her heart pounded harder; the pull of the impending Change became much more insistent the closer they drew to the woods. She tugged on Gage's hand as fear locked up her feet, and they came to a stop.

"What if I'm not ready?" she whispered to Gage as he cupped her face.

He stroked her cheek with the back of his hand. "None of us thinks we're ready the first time because there is no way to prepare for what's about to happen. We can tell you about it and you can read others' accounts, but it's still unlike anything you could ever have imagined. Just know this"—he placed his forehead against hers and held her gaze—"you are strong enough to do this. You are a queen of wolves, and one of the toughest women I know. Nothing can break you."

She stared into his eyes and felt the strength of his confidence in her. The tremble in her bones never went away completely, but it soothed some once it was comforted by Gage's love and encouragement.

"Okay," she rasped, nodding her head once.

They walked hand in hand silently through the woods. Gage chuckled. "Careful. You'll cut off my circulation."

"Gosh, I'm sorry," she said, easing her grip. "My

stomach is doing a number on me."

"It's okay," he said with a smile, though he looked a bit uneasy himself. "Everyone's nervous their first time."

Danica snorted.

"No sexual innuendos intended," Gage corrected in a smoky voice that made her laugh.

They spoke easily about different things for the rest of the short walk to the clearing. A lake stretched before them, and the water glittered under the moonlight.

Gage set down the bag with their necessities. He faced her and took a deep breath, grasping both of her hands. His heart was beating as fast as her own; she could feel his pulse through their fingers and the flitter of his nerves through their mating bond. "Ready?"

Danica swallowed hard, finding it difficult to do so because her throat had nearly closed up. Unable to speak, she mutely nodded and began undressing.

Her fingers fumbled with the buttons on her blouse, her clammy hands missing the holes over and over. Gage at last steadied her fingers and guided her actions. "It's okay," he said gently as they tackled the line of buttons together. "It'll be over before you know it."

"I'm scared," she whispered as her top came off. He started on her blue jeans next.

"I know. I wish I could spare you this. If there were a way to break the bond—"

She placed a finger to his lips. "Don't ever say that. Nothing in this world or the next could tear me from you. If going through this means keeping you, then I'll endure any hell."

"Danica—"

"Ssssh." She stood on her tiptoes and lightly pressed her lips to his.

He kissed her back, the tender gesture quickly deepening into something fiery. Gage broke off the kiss and groaned deep in his throat. "Hmmm…. More time for that later."

"Or now," she murmured, starting to kiss him again.

"Danica…."

"Fine, fine." She shimmied out of the rest of her clothes, feeling far too exposed in nothing but her skin. It wasn't exactly warm tonight. Fall was banging on summer's door, and goose bumps prickled along her skin. Her nipples perked from the chill.

Their bodies were cloaked in shadows. They stood just along the edge of the forest, out of the circle of moonlight bathing the meadow.

Gage undressed quickly. She couldn't take her eyes off him the entire time; she let her eyes rove over the finely sculpted abs and the threaded muscles along her arms, legs, and chest. He was beautiful.

And he was all hers.

Her eyes dropped to the erection jutting between his legs, and heat surged beneath her belly button. More than anything, she wanted to mount him right then and there.

He followed her gaze, his eyes flashing gold with desire. "Soon," he murmured, kissing her neck as he slowly turned her around so her back was to him. Her eyes immediately fixed on the moonlight, and a new hunger took over. It was as if every nerve in her body had come alive with electric tingles that set her heart to racing. Her fear took a backseat to her desire to become one with the moonlight, to change into something more feral.

"Step into the light," Gage whispered into her ear.

Danica took a deep breath, steadying herself mentally, and stepped forward. Grass tickled her feet, and tall, purple flowers kissed her bare thighs as she pressed forward, one step at a time. Her heart beat harder with every breath she took, until all she could hear was the sound of her excitement beating away in her chest.

The sounds of the crickets and owls died away as she paused on the edge of light and closed her eyes.

*Just breathe.*

Then she stepped forward.

The second the light hit her, she felt the Change take hold. With a cry, she buckled over as fire melted her bones and stretched her skin so taut she thought it would rip clean off. She screamed, the sound of her human voice morphing into a ghoulish, high-pitched howl.

Distantly, she heard Gage yelling out instructions to her, but she could barely make out what he was saying. All she could focus on was pain, pain, pain and praying the agony would end.

At last, the fiery hell ended. It washed away, leaving her filled with a sense of euphoria unlike anything she'd ever felt before. Sounds she hadn't noticed as a human fought for her attention; the scuttle of ants moving along the dirt, of earthworms burrowing tunnels in the soil far below her, of predators soaring through the open sky above.

Slowly, she opened her eyes. Good God, everything

was so much *sharper*. Had she been blind as a human?

*Danica.*

She turned, clumsily righting herself as she adjusted to spreading her weight over four large paws. A great white wolf with vibrant blue eyes came up beside her.

Her mate.

He sniffed her with his big black nose and whimpered. *Are you all right?*

*I'm... more than all right. I'm amazing.*

He opened up his mouth, panting and making it look like he was smiling as his red tongue lolled over the side of his fangs. *Take a look in the lake.*

She did as he said and stepped forward. Slowly, the sight of a golden wolf came into view on the water's surface, its green eyes glowing with flecks of gold.

*Wow*, she breathed. *Is that... is that really me?*

*You're beautiful*, Gage said, coming up beside her. *Something else, isn't it?*

*It's indescribable.*

*Want to give your new body a test drive?* he said eagerly, pawing at the dirt like a dog that wanted to be thrown a ball.

She yipped. *Hell yeah, I do!*

With that, Gage took off and she chased after him. They flew over the forest ground, her confidence in her new self growing the more she ran, leapt, and sprang. Wind raked through her fur, and she howled with the ecstasy of feeling so free and powerful.

Gage and she played tag with one another, running the full length of the forest and coming back again around dawn to the spot where she'd first shed her human skin and evolved into a full-fledged werewolf.

As the sky lightened and the moon set, her skin tingled with the familiar itch that had started it all. Though it hurt to turn back—but not as much as the first time she'd turned into a wolf—she found herself sad to be going back to her human form. As a wolf, she didn't have to worry about bills or politics or any of the other day-to-day bullshit she dealt with. She was just... free.

The sun had barely broken the horizon when she finished changing back, and the two of them sprawled across the grass, sweating and panting as the golden light crept across the meadow.

She shivered as the sunlight warmed her skin, already missing the moon that had given her the greatest gift she'd ever known.

Gage opened the bag he'd brought and got out a blanket. They cuddled in it, and she leaned her head on his shoulder as they watched the sun rise. She'd been so scared before, but now a remarkable sense of peace filled her. She smiled softly.

A new day—and a new chapter in her life—was beginning.

*A brighter chapter.*

"It's been a long time since I've done this," Gage murmured against her hair.

She snuggled into him, enjoying the scent of pine and nature. Now that she'd shifted once, her senses remained somewhat sharpened in human form, but she still felt like she couldn't quite breathe because it was all so much to take in. "Me too."

"My brothers and I used to climb up on the barn and watch the sun rise over the farm all the time."

She blinked. "You lived on a farm?"

He nodded, a wistful yet sad look in his eyes. "We lived in the slums in the city when I was very little, but my father had always loved the countryside. So we moved to the boonies when I was a bit older. We were veritable country bumpkins, complete with cows, goats, and chickens. My favorite was the horses. They could run like the wind."

"Why don't you have horses now?" she asked. They certainly had the money for them.

Gage shrugged. "Not enough time to take care of them properly."

After a quiet moment, she said gently, "Do you miss that life?"

"Sometimes," he admitted. "It was simpler." Then he looked at her affectionately and kissed the top of her head. "But I can't say I'd rather be anywhere else."

She held his gaze, pulling his head back toward hers. "Me either," she whispered against his lips.

They kissed, their tongues lightly dancing along one another's. His hand slipped up to tangle in her windblown hair, and she wrapped her arms around his neck, loving the way her already erect nipples rubbed against his chest.

Her inner wolf was restless from earlier. She'd thought about making love while they were both in wolf form, but she wasn't quite that bold yet. The more human part of her—the woman who was madly in love with her man—craved human touch.

She gently grabbed his other hand and guided it to one of her breasts. He cupped it, squeezing and kneading and teasing the nipple as she climbed onto his lap, straddling him. Her honey coated his thickening shaft as she ground against him, the fire below her belly building with every scintillating stroke. He groaned and picked her up, keeping the blanket wrapped around them as he planted her back against a tree. She could feel the contour of the bark, but it wasn't rough, not with the soft padding of the thick blanket to protect her skin.

A moment later when Gage entered her, she didn't notice much of anything else anyway.

She moaned as he began pumping, and she wrapped her legs around him. Her nails dug into his back as his hips bucked harder, making love to her with an urgency and a wildness that made her blood boil with desire.

The pleasure built quickly, ending with her crying out his name as he grunted. He pumped a few more times before they were both spent.

He held her up, both of them drenched in sweat and panting, their hot breath mingling with each other's.

"I love you," he said, staring into her eyes.

She smiled. It wasn't the first time he'd told her, but she'd never tire of hearing it. People had rarely told her so much.

"I love you too," she rasped, smiling, and kissed him again.

They kissed sweetly for a while as the sunlight grew, turning everything gold. At last, he set her down and reached into the bag to glance at his phone. He scanned through a text message and looked at the clock on the app screen. "It's almost six. What do you say we order room service and spend the morning in bed?"

"You don't have any meetings?"

"Not until two. Alara texted me and said I might have a panel this afternoon if chosen as a candidate. That leaves my morning free. So unless the palace catches on fire, I don't plan on leaving your side."

She smiled widely. "Sounds good to me."

It was rare they got to spend a day together. He kissed her again and got out a bottle of wipes from the bag, as well as a towel and a clean change of clothes.

She took a wipe and began swiping it across her sweaty body.

Still riding the endorphin high from her orgasm, she didn't notice the warning at first. Slowly, an uncomfortable pressure built inside her head, rising until finally something snapped, and she gasped in pain.

Gage growled, closing his eyes as his face scrunched up. "Jesus. What the—?" His voice choked as he stared at her shoulders. Every drop of blood drained from his face as his eyes widened. "Oh, my God."

"What?" Danica said, still reeling from whatever the hell had made her brain hurt. "What is it?"

She looked down. At first it didn't register what the big deal was.

It hit her with the force of a two-by-four. "Holy shit," she breathed. She looked at Gage's shoulders and then examined her own skin again, just to be sure.

Their mating tattoos were gone.

*Don't. Panic.*

No matter how many times he said it to himself, Gage couldn't shake the rising horror in his chest. Something was terribly wrong.

"Come on. Let's find Alara and have her contact a witch to see what's wrong."

They dressed quickly and practically jogged toward the palace.

"What do you think happened?" Danica said, worry written all over her pretty face. She looked so lovely with her cheeks flushed from their lovemaking.

A moment that was now shattered by his mounting terror.

"I don't know," he said. "Some side effect of the Change, perhaps. I've never seen anything like this before, nor have I heard of it. There has to be some explanation."

He took her hand and kissed the back of it. "I'll make it right, I swear."

He hoped he wasn't giving her empty promises. The night he'd taken her as a mate, he'd sworn never to let her down.

But what could he do when he had no idea what he was up against? How could he hope to fight an unseen enemy?

*There has to be a way to fix it. There has to be.*

Not wanting to draw unwanted attention, especially considering all the extra guests the castle was currently housing, he guided her toward the back through the hedge-row maze. They wound through the paths, racing toward the castle.

All the while he reached through their mental connection to get a feel on his mate's emotions to make sure she was all right, and became increasingly frustrated when he found nothing there. It was as if he was groping in the darkness, reaching for a bond that never existed. He suddenly felt incredibly lonely.

"Gage," Danica said, and his heart broke at the unshed tears he heard in her voice. "I can't feel you."

"I know. It's okay, baby. We'll fix it."

*Run. Go faster.*

His heart raced and he struggled to calm his panic. They were almost at the kitchen entrance when a dark figure stepped from around the bend, and Gage yanked Danica behind him.

Gage snarled. "What are you doing here?"

Malachite, clad in a black silk shirt and black dress pants, stood there. His eyes swept over Gage in dismissal before resting on Danica with acute interest. "Good morning, my lady. Did you rest well?"

Gage stepped forward. "I said, 'what the hell are you doing here?'"

Malachite tore his eyes off Danica and gave Gage a malicious smile.

"I'm here to challenge you for your mate."

# CHAPTER EIGHT

GAGE STARED AT HIM. "HAVE YOU LOST YOUR DAMN mind?"

Malachite raised a brow, nonplussed. "Should I repeat myself?"

"I heard what you said," Gage snapped. "That doesn't change the fact that what you're suggesting is impossible."

"Impossible or just unheard of?"

Gage could feel the tips of his claws digging into his palms, itching to take a piece out of that sadistic son of a bitch. "Look, I don't know what your interest in Danica is, but I will die before I let you near her."

Malachite frowned. "I assure you I have no intention of harming her."

"Well, you'll excuse me if I don't believe you, given your previous track record with relationships—or lack thereof."

Malachite almost look stricken before schooling his

features once more. "The pack—"

"Save it. I've heard enough of your excuses." Taking Danica's hand, he quickly rushed by Malachite.

Malachite caught Danica's wrist, his eyes pleading. "Please, Danica, hear me out." His eyes shifted to her shoulder, and he squinted. His eyes widened. "It worked," he murmured.

Gage narrowed his eyes at him. "What worked?"

Malachite continued staring at her skin, reaching up to lift the collar of her shirt.

With a growl, Gage snatched his hand away and pushed Danica behind him. "Don't touch her." He grabbed a fistful of Malachite's shirt, getting right in his face. "Tell me what you know. What's happened to us? Are you the one responsible for our missing tattoos?"

Malachite gripped Gage's hand, his eyes searching and hopeful. "They're gone? Truly?"

Gage blinked, taken aback. "What have you done, Malachite?" he whispered.

Malachite stared at him, then looked again at Danica. "Can you feel him?"

"What?" she snapped.

"Your mate. Can you feel him?"

Danica hesitated, shifting her weight and looking at Gage in question.

Malachite's eyes flashed in surprise before he chuckled darkly. "My, my, my. So the old wolf still has a few tricks up his sleeve after all."

Gage's eyes narrowed and flared gold. He grabbed two fistfuls of Malachite's freshly pressed shirt. "What. Have.

You. Done?"

That arrogant smirk returned to Malachite's face, the same look he'd given Gage all those years when Gage had endured living under his rule. "*I* haven't done anything," Malachite said.

Gage's anger began to simmer. "Then somebody did. What was it?"

"Wouldn't you like to know?"

It was such a childish thing to say that Gage's thin hold over his temper snapped. His knuckles itched for another piece of Malachite's face. Before Gage had time to fully think through the consequences of his actions, his fist flew out.

Malachite was prepared. With predatory grace, he shifted his head to the side and avoided the blow.

"Gage!" Danica shrieked, grabbing hold of his arm before he could pull back and fire off another punch. "What are you doing?"

"I'm sick of him," Gage seethed. "Just the mere sight of him fills me with rage."

Regret briefly flashed through Malachite's eyes before that glacial indifference returned. "Soon it won't matter how you feel because I'll be long gone—as soon as I get what I came for." He looked at Danica and she froze.

Gage bared his fangs, growling. "Don't look at my mate like that, you piece of shit."

"But she's not really your mate anymore, is she?" Malachite asked, cocking his head.

"What are you talking about?"

"The tattoos." He gestured at the unmarked flesh on

both their shoulders. "They're gone."

"It doesn't mean anything," Gage insisted, feeling his stomach churn.

Malachite smiled cruelly. "What if it does? What if it means you're not worthy of her?"

"Of course he is," Danica snapped, her beautiful face flush with anger. "He's the only one for me."

Malachite eyed her. "How many men have you been with? One, two at the most?"

She blinked. "I—that's none of your business!"

"What if the Mark was a mistake? What if your true mate is standing right before you?"

They both stared at him.

"You mean *you*?" Danica blurted.

"Yes," Malachite answered unwaveringly.

"This is absurd," Gage spat, taking Danica's hand. "We're not listening to any more of your lies." He tried shoving past Malachite, but he caught hold of Danica's wrist. She was trapped between the two werewolves, one clinging to either hand.

Gage growled, stalking forward. "When I say don't touch her, that's exactly what I mean—don't fucking touch her."

"What if she doesn't want to leave with you?" Malachite said, his eyes darkening in challenge.

"Actually, I do," Danica said, trying to jerk free. "So let up, pal."

Malachite's grip remained firm. "Danica—"

"You know," Gage said, "I'm getting really tired of your shit. I was tired of it a long time ago, but I wasn't in a position to do anything about it. But now, things have changed. I'm the Alpha now, and you're just some prick who thinks he's above it all. Well, you know what? I kicked your ass once, and by God, I can do it again." He cracked his knuckles. "This time, I'm going to enjoy it."

He led with another punch. As predicted, Malachite started to dart to the side to avoid it, but Gage followed up with a second punch. He drove his fist squarely into Malachite's chest. The air rushed from the wolf's lungs as his eyes went wide in shock.

Gage grinned. "Who's the bitch now?"

Malachite recovered quickly as his eyes blazed bright gold. "You insolent whelp. I should have killed you when I had the chance."

He charged, and the two men began exchanging blows in a flurry of movements.

Danica watched from the sideline, screaming at them to stop. "You're going to kill each other! Knock it off right now!"

Gage barely heard her. Well, her scared voice registered in his head, but all he could think was, *Protect, protect, protect.* He'd felt helpless to protect his father when the scorned werewolf came and destroyed their lives, marking them with the Curse of the Moon. He wouldn't fail to protect one of the few cherished people he had left.

With the numbness of adrenaline coursing through his veins, Gage barely felt Malachite's blows. He vaguely felt his flesh being ripped apart by claws and felt his bones rattle with every blow Malachite managed to land, but still he fought.

*I can't lose her. I* have *to win.*

"Gage! GAGE!"

From behind him, a man shouted his name. A moment later, strong arms were hooked around his, hauling him off a bloodied and bruised Malachite.

Malachite started forward, eyes narrowed in rage, but the man holding Gage shouted, "Stand down!"

Still Malachite charged—until Danica stepped in front of him. She held her arms out, blocking his path.

"Stop!" she screamed. "Enough. No more fighting. I'm not going to have you fighting over me."

Malachite stopped and stared down at her with mixed emotions on his face.

Her shoulders heaved. Though she hadn't fought, she was breathing just as heavily as they were. "I've made my choice and it's Gage. Malachite, you can't make someone love you."

Malachite's face fell. The sadness in his eyes betrayed his emotions. "Then I shall have to prove to you I'm someone worthy of your love."

Turning on his heel, he strode away and disappeared around a corner.

Gage fought his captor, who was still holding him hostage. "He's getting away!"

Suddenly, he was spun around just in time for a hand to fly across his face. The force of the slap stunned him, scrambling his thoughts for a moment. Reeling from the flare of white-hot pain on his cheek, his vision focused on the man who'd pulled him off Malachite.

"Nik?"

His brother stood there with his arms crossed, surrounded by a group of bystanders who watched Gage with wide, malicious smiles. He hadn't realized he'd had an audience; he'd been so lost in his bloodlust.

Nik looked like he could choke someone. Namely Gage, whom he leveled his glare at. "Inside. *Now*."

Just like when they were kids, Nik took hold of him and marched through the crowd. They chuckled as the brothers and Danica passed.

"Bastards," she muttered under her breath. "They wouldn't even help stop the fight."

"That's because they were probably hoping they'd tear each other apart," Nik said wearily. "Word's spread about you running for king. You've spooked them because they're afraid the Council will favor you." He glared at Gage. "But not if you keep up this bullshit."

"I wasn't—"

"Save it. Not here."

Gage's jaw ticked as he pressed his mouth shut. He jerked his arm free, walking ahead of Nik with Danica trailing behind.

He couldn't look at his mate. He was still too worked up. Why the hell did Malachite affect him like this? Why couldn't he control his anger, bitterness, and hatred every time he saw him?

*Some people leave a mark on the soul.*

Malachite's reign had left a lot of emotional and physical scars.

Wounds Gage obviously hadn't healed from.

Nik waited until they were back in Gage and Danica's

room before turning on him. "Have you lost your mind! Do you want to sink your chances of winning before you've even had a chance to fight for the crown?"

"I didn't ask for this!" Gage shouted. Danica hovered near the wall, staying out of it. She watched the brothers nervously.

"No, you didn't," Nik said, running a hand over his short-cropped hair. "But you did make the choice to run for king, so you damn well better take this seriously."

His brother's scorn hurt. "I am taking it seriously."

"No, you're not. If you were, you wouldn't fly off the handle every time Malachite looks at you the wrong way."

"It wasn't me he was looking at," Gage said bitterly, casting his mate a glance.

Nik turned, doing a double-take as he caught sight of Danica's shoulders. He looked at Gage, pulling his shirt back and searching his skin. "Where are your tattoos?"

Gage sighed and launched into a condensed version of what happened. "Next thing we knew, Malachite cornered us and started rambling about claiming Danica as his own."

"He can't do that, can he?" Danica asked with a tremor in her voice. She looked fearfully between them.

"Sssh," Gage said, pulling her to him and kissing the top of her head. "If Malachite thinks he can take you from me, he's delusional." It drove him nuts that he couldn't sense her emotions. Sometimes her fear was comforting because it reminded him he wasn't alone.

"Malachite, delusional?" Nik said with mock surprise. "And here I thought he was such a sensible son of a bitch."

Gage couldn't help but crack a smile at his brother's attempt at lightening the mood. "There can't be any truth to his threat. He's just trying to shake me up. From the sound of it, he was working with someone else."

"Probably a competitor for the crown," Nik murmured, stroking the stubble along his chin. If anyone could make "scruffy" stylish, it was Nik. "All the same, it's strange your tattoos vanished. I'll find Alara and have her bring in a witch to do some magical analysis since the marks are summoned by magic." He started to turn. "Oh, and try not to kick anyone else's ass for the next fifteen minutes, hmmm?"

Gage smirked and nodded.

Nik left and Danica shuddered.

Gage stroked her hair, still holding her. "What are you thinking of?"

She started to sob.

"Hey," he said gently, brows furrowing as he crooked his index finger under her chin and lifted her head. "What's wrong?"

"The fact you have to ask tears me apart," she blubbered. "You used to be able to know how I was feeling without asking. I feel empty and lost inside. I miss you, Gage. I miss you so much."

He tucked her head against his chest as she cried. "I'm not going anywhere. Don't let what he said scare you."

"But what if he's not bluffing? What if he really does have a way to take me away from you?"

"That's not going to happen," Gage growled. "No matter what, I swear I'll die before I let you go. You understand?"

She hiccupped and nodded, her hysteria dimming.

He clutched her, an ominous warning stirring in the back of his head.

Like the battle was only just beginning.

# CHAPTER NINE

**D**ANICA FELT READY TO SCREAM.

True to her word, Alara had sent her best witch to them ASAP. She spent about thirty minutes scrying and puzzling and chanting before scratching her head and saying, "I'll need to consult my peers on this," and then she left.

Danica knew it was just another way of saying, "I don't have a damn clue what the hell is wrong with you."

"What the hell does that even mean?" Danica asked after the witch left. "That 'the magic feels normal?' There is nothing 'normal' about being a werewolf!"

"Calm down, love," Gage said, resting his hands on her shoulders.

"How can I calm down?" she shrieked. "I just had the most exhilarating night of my life, and just when I think things are finally settling into place, something like this slaps me in the face! I'm sick of it!" Her shoulders shook with contained sobs, and she rested her forehead against his chest, trying to keep it together. Dammit, why did she have to cry every time she got mad? "I feel like such a mess and I'm so… tired of it all. Tired of the drama and the lies and the secrets. I just want to be with you. Why is that so hard for the universe to understand?"

"Then be with me," Gage said, cupping her cheek. "Who cares what a stupid tattoo means? I love you. Do you love me?"

"Yes," she answered without hesitation.

He kissed her head. "Then that's all that matters. Let the rest of the world figure out what it means. I made you a promise, Danica, that no one—and I mean, no one—would ever take you from me, and I plan on keeping it."

She hugged him, the strength of his conviction chasing away some of her fears. Gage was always so strong and self-assured, while she felt like her emotions were all over the place. Danica had wanted to tell the witch that "normal" felt "awful" and not right at all. Ever since the bond had snapped, she'd felt as if a piece of herself had gone missing, and her body—her very soul—ached to get it back.

She'd just about sell a limb to feel that connected to Gage again. She just felt so… empty.

Someone gently cleared their throat behind them, and the couple turned.

Alara stood there patiently, looking lovely in a crisp, clean business suit, though it was barely sunrise. "I hate to interrupt, but Gage, you have your panel before the Council this morning. You've been chosen as one of the candidates."

He blinked in surprise. "I thought they weren't announcing the candidates until two?"

"Apparently they only thought five of you were worthy and wanted to get on with things. Thus, they're having messengers privately tell each chosen candidate this morning. They are also pushing all the panels up on the schedule to get things going."

He frowned. "You said I have a panel *this morning*?"

"Yes."

He glanced at Danica and then the bed. "I thought you said if I was chosen, the panel would be this afternoon?"

"Like I said, they made a change in the schedules and decided to have you go first."

He arched a brow, annoyed. "And who is this 'they' you keep speaking of?"

"The Council, of course."

"Well, what the hell is their problem? Why are they so impatient?"

Her tone cooled a few degrees. "I don't know. But I suspect it has something to do with the witch mafia threat hanging over our heads." She leveled her gaze at him. Alara was not a woman to be cowed by anyone. "You forget that though I am regent here, my power on that Council is irrelevant. They are above us all in rank and power. And I don't have enough political sway to begin to ask them why they do what they do."

"Sorry," he said, running a hand through his hair. "I didn't mean to jump down your throat. It's just been a long morning."

She looked at him sympathetically. "I can understand. And had I any way to postpone this, I would."

"Right." He looked at Danica and squeezed her hand. "Don't worry. Everything will be fine. I'm sure that witch will do everything she can to get us right again."

Danica tried smiling at him as he kissed her on the cheek and left with Nik, but it felt like her mouth wouldn't work.

Alara lingered. "You know, there's a last-minute gala they decided to host tomorrow night to celebrate the candidates. The Council will even be there. Do you have a dress?"

Danica recognized a ploy to distract her when she saw one. She couldn't deny that it was welcome and hadn't come soon enough.

She laughed. "Honestly, getting all dressed up is the least of my worries right now."

"Understandably so." Alara's eyes sparkled with mischief as she pressed her lips together, thinking. She took Danica's hand and started for the door.

"What the—? Hey, where are we going?" Danica yelped.

"To my room. I might have something you could wear." She looked Danica up and down. "We're about the same size."

Well, that was wishful thinking, as Danica found out. To her dismay, Alara was a bit smaller than her. The dresses, while beautiful, gathered at the wrong spots and clung to her curves a little too much. That is, if she could even get them zipped up.

Disappointed and feeling bad about her curves, Danica stared forlornly at her reflection in the mirror, wearing yet another dress that didn't fit.

Alara came up behind her and smiled, a determined look coming over her face. "All right, so much for that idea. Come on, get changed and put your shoes back on."

"Why?" Danica asked, raising her brows.

"We're getting you out of here," Alara said with a devious smile. "The boys will be indisposed for a while, and I'd say us girls have earned a little, well, 'girl time.'"

"Girl time?"

Alara grinned. "*We* are going dress shopping."

"Is anywhere open?" Danica said, surprised. "It's barely daylight out."

"I know of a place that opens early and closes early," Alara said with an excited sparkle in her eyes. "It's in a small town near here, and you know how small towns tend to run on their own schedules."

Oh, Danica knew all too well. "Normal business hours" in Moonstruck meant anything from 5 a.m. to 2 p.m. or 5 p.m. to midnight and so on. Most of the shops had been locally owned and run by the owners themselves, so they could do whatever they pleased.

Danica couldn't deny that getting out of the castle sounded wonderful right now. Despite the fact she wanted to cling to Gage like a spider monkey and never let go, she let Alara pull her back to her room, where she showered and dressed before they left in the most expensive car Danica had ever ridden in.

Alara brought along two bodyguards, both of which

sat in the back since Alara had insisted on driving "her baby."

A symphonic metal band Danica had never heard before filtered through the radio speakers. The singer had a lovely, lilting voice that soared over the deep undertones of the bass and guitars. The song was haunting and sad, just the kind of tune her soul needed to heal right now. "These guys are pretty good," she said.

"I think they're called Black Rose," Alara replied idly. "They're an indie band that popped up a few months ago. Since they're all paranormals, they're starting to become pretty popular in the Underworld, and among human audiences."

Danica blinked, surprised. *Imagine that. A werewolf/ witch/whatever-they-were rock band.* "Cool."

The engine roared as Alara gunned the pedal. Danica's teeth ground together as her heart rate shot up.

"What is this anyway?" Danica said, gripping the door handle as Alara took a curve with breathtaking speed. The blood-red car easily hugged the curve and surged forward on the open country road, its engine roaring like an angry lion.

"It's a Mitsubishi Firestorm. They named it that because you'll burn up the road in this bad boy." Alara grinned from ear to ear. "Pretty cool, huh?"

*Pretty dangerous.* Danica was too scared to look at the speedometer. "Yeah," she lied through gritted teeth. "Pretty bad. I've never heard of them."

"That's because there aren't many models," she said matter-of-factly. "It's a prototype. My father had a love for fast cars, a love which he passed down to me. Although, I guess he wasn't really my father." Her face scrunched up in a painful wince.

Danica watched her silently for a moment. "I'm sorry."

Alara blinked and recovered. "For what?" she said aloofly.

"For the whole baby-daddy drama. It wasn't right of him to treat you that way." God, she had no idea what she'd do if her father had tried sacrificing her to some demonic witch. Forget the family drama—that shit was messed up.

Alara's face hardened. "I was glad he did. It reminded me I can't trust anyone in my world."

"You can trust Nik, though," Danica insisted softly.

Alara pressed her lips together. "I know."

Danica studied her. "But you're scared to." She sighed, resting her head back on the seat. "I know that feeling. When everyone in your life lets you down, it can be hard to let go of that distrust. You come to rely only on your-self." She smiled sadly. "But let me tell you from experi-ence—*that* gets pretty lonely."

Alara's gaze grew heavy. "Sometimes you're better off alone."

"You can't mean that," Danica chided gently. "I see the way you look at Nik."

Alara's face lit up with that warm, loving glow Danica had seen on her own since meeting Gage. "Yeah. Much as it scares me to admit it, I love him. With all my heart. What's left of it, anyway."

Danica reached over and squeezed her hand. "You'll heal with time."

"I hope so," Alara whispered.

Danica decided to shift the topic onto something relatively mindless. "Seen any good movies lately?"

Alara blushed. "I've never actually been to a movie theater."

Danica stared at her, waiting for her to say she was joking. "Like, never ever?"

Alara nodded.

"Oh. My. God. Girl, we have got to get you out more."

"My parents would never allow it, with me being the crown princess and all. My father thought it would be too much of a security risk. Not that that matters anymore," she added bitterly. "I pretty much grew up in the castle."

Danica's shoulders slumped. It sounded so sad, like a lion who had grown up in a cage in a zoo. Animals like that weren't meant to be caged—they were meant to be free. "Bummer. Remind me when this is all over to show you what the world is really like. It can be fun."

Alara brightened up. "I'd like that."

They made easy conversation the rest of the way, eventually ending up in a surprisingly chic mall in a town about fifteen minutes from the castle.

Danica saw more guards in disguise watching them in the parking lot. Some talked on cell phones, others pretended to be fellow shoppers walking into the mall…. They all looked so alarmingly *normal*. On the ride, Danica had asked Alara if they needed more guards. Alara had snorted and said, "Hardly. See that beat-up Camry behind us? And that mini-van ahead of us? Both are full of guards in disguise. There will be more once we get to the mall.

Seriously, I have eyes everywhere."

Alara hadn't been kidding. Now that she knew what to look for, Danica counted at least twenty men and women who were on Alara's personal security team, and that was just on the outside of the mall. Danica wouldn't be surprised to see an army once they got inside.

"No offense, but I'm surprised you can find a mall this nice in a town this size," Danica said as they went inside, trying not to think of all the eyeballs on her. Though it made her feel more secure to be watched by so many guards, it also unnerved her a bit.

"This town might be small, but it has a lot of old and new money in it. It's a very wealthy community, actually," Alara said as they walked through the mall, trailed by her bodyguards. They had ditched the formal castle-guard attire in favor of jeans, sneakers, and T-shirts. Alara said they were supposed to be their "boyfriends."

"No kidding," Danica said, eyeing the marble floor, pristine fountains, and modern architecture. The mall had all the mainstream stores she was used to seeing—Forever 21, Charlotte Russe, Old Navy—but Alara pulled her into a shop she had never heard of before called The Dress Boutique. It was cute and cozy, with racks and racks of beautiful gowns.

"This is where I buy all my dresses," Alara said. "They specialize in women with a little extra girth."

"Sounds like my kind of store." Danica idly picked up a price tag and her eyes nearly bugged out of her head. "Holy shit, this dress is five hundred dollars!"

"So?"

"So I can't afford that! Well, technically I can, since Gage and I share a bank account now, but that's still a lot of money to pay for just a dress!"

Alara smiled. "Then let me get it."

Danica's eyes bugged. "No! I couldn't let you do that."

"Please." Alara smiled warmly and placed a hand on Danica's arm. "It's the least I can do for you after you saved Nik's life back at that ghetto-licious hotel."

Danica snorted. "Did you just say 'ghetto-licious?'"

"See?" Alara said proudly. "You *can* teach an old wolf new tricks. Before long, I shall sound just as hip and trendy as the rest of you."

About then, a clerk sashayed over. "Hello, Ms. Crescent! How can I help you? Back for another ball gown?" she said eagerly, no doubt licking her lips over the generous commission she'd receive.

"Actually, I'm here to get a dress for my friend. This is Danica. Danica, Suzie. She's marvelous and helps me pick out all my gowns."

"Hello!" Suzie gushed, grabbing Danica's hand and shaking it with so much fervor that Danica's teeth rattled. "I'm so delighted to meet one of Alara's friends!"

Danica smiled with effort. *I bet you are, since it means more money for you.* "Nice to meet you," she said with stiff politeness.

Suzie immediately seized Danica and tugged her into a dressing room. "With your complexion, I think pastels will wash you out. We need something that will contrast with that lovely pale-blond hair."

"You don't say?"

Suzie shooed her toward the awaiting dressing room. "Go ahead and strip, and I'll start bringing you gowns."

"But don't I get to pick them out?"

Suzie stared at her like she was slow. "Of course. You get to pick from the ones *I* choose for you to try on." She slammed the door in Danica's face, and Danica blinked.

"Well then, okay, crazy," she grumbled and began undressing. She'd just stripped down to the essentials when the door opened and in walked Suzie with an armload of dresses.

"Jeez, don't you knock!" Danica said, trying to cover herself.

"Oh, honey, you don't have anything I haven't seen before. Come on. Pick a dress and come out so we can see it."

Outside the door was a wraparound mirror, a dais for girls to stand on and twirl, and some fancy chairs. Alara sat in one, watching Danica with an amused smirk. She giggled as Danica glared at Suzie and mouthed, "Crazy," before shutting the door and locking it this time.

Danica wasn't so sure about Suzie before, but after flipping through the dresses she'd brought her, she had to admit the woman knew what she was talking about. The dresses were all gorgeous and tasteful, and every single one looked great on Danica. She was shy at first to show them off, but she quickly got into the "dress up" game and eagerly twirled for Alara and Suzie.

"That autumn orange one is stunning," Suzie said.

"I prefer the dark red," Alara said, eyeing the red dress Danica currently had on. "It screams old Hollywood elegance. With a chignon, some chandelier earrings, and some lipstick to match, she would be exquisite."

"Yes, yes," Suzie murmured, her eyes sparkling. "Oh, I have the perfect shoes to match. Do you want to look at the earrings, dear?"

Danica blinked. "Me?"

"Yes, you!" Suzie huffed. "Who else would I be talking to?"

"Well," Danica said carefully, "it's just that you haven't asked me to pick out anything yet."

"Well, you can't screw up the earrings," Suzie said, as if this should be obvious, and waddled off.

Alara gave her an apologetic smile, shrugging as if to say, "That's Suzie," before following after the saleswoman.

Danica sighed, gathered her skirts, and walked into the main store. Alara pointed her in the direction of the jewelry, which was off in a separate room. Being the middle of the day and the middle of the work week, there weren't many people in the mall. They were the only guests in the store, and the jewelry room was empty.

Danica's jaw dropped as she entered. The room sparkled with a myriad of multi-colored gems. She felt like she'd stepped inside a bright, sparkly rainbow. Most of the earrings were on rotating black velvet racks that pitched dainty lights along the walls.

Her heart leapt to her throat as she eyed the price tags. The dresses didn't have anything on the jewelry when it came to being expensive. No way could she let Alara cover the earrings too.

Hoping Gage would take, "She didn't leave me any choice," as an excuse, Danica looked at the chandelier earrings on display.

She felt someone lean in behind her. "You look radiant," said a deep, masculine voice beside her ear.

She yelped and whirled, clutching the vanity. "Malachite," she breathed.

He stood there looking devilishly handsome in a buccaneer kind of way, wearing a brown leather trench coat, a pirate shirt, dark jeans, and boots. His silver-blond hair was pulled halfway back at the nape of his neck, making his Arthurian face seem much more angular and lean. Even she had to admit it was a good look on him.

Malachite smiled, which made him look even more stunning with his perfectly straight, white teeth. "You remembered my name."

Danica's eyes narrowed. "Hard to forget the name of the man who made my mate's life a living hell."

That knocked the glow right off his face. "I was a different man then."

Danica pursed her lips and crossed her arms. "What are you doing here?"

"Shopping."

"Stalking," Danica coughed.

Malachite didn't deny it. While it was nice to have the attention of such an attractive man, the fact he was pure evil kind of ruined it for her. "Don't you have puppies to choke?" she said, giving him a frosty smile that said, "Get lost."

He stared at her with such sadness, she was almost sorry she'd been a bitch.

*Almost.*

"Do you really think me to be so vile?" he asked.

"If you're trying to win me over with this whole 'hot pirate' getup," she said, gesturing to his outfit, "and those sad eyes, it's not going to work." She started to move around him when he caught her wrist.

"Wait. Please." He stared at her hand and his frown deepened. "I don't understand."

It took her a moment to catch on to what had upset him. "What?" She jerked her hand free. "Disappointed you didn't mark me? Sorry, it's because you're *not my mate*."

"But you are unmarked."

"And it doesn't mean a damn thing!" she screamed, fisting the skirt in her hands to keep from hauling off and hitting him. "I love Gage, end of story!"

Malachite's jaw dropped, like she'd knocked the wind from him. He swallowed hard and ducked his head. "Am I really so despicable to you that the thought of loving me disgusts you so?"

Her anger ebbed, replaced by the teeniest bit of guilt. For a moment, he almost seemed… *human*.

She growled a sigh and crossed her arms. "Look, I'm sorry. But actions speak louder than words, and you have a history of being kind of a dick."

His head shot up. "I can change."

"Then show us," she said. "If you've changed so much, prove to the others you're a different man."

"I could be for you."

She closed her eyes and counted to ten. "Stop it. I don't know what you've gotten in your head, but this infatuation with claiming me or whatever it is you hope to do has got to stop."

"I could make you happy. I know I could." He took a step toward her. "Danica—"

His gaze cut to her chest suddenly, widening. "Get down!"

# CHAPTER TEN

ASTER THAN SHE COULD FOLLOW, HE GRABBED HOLD OF her and shoved her to the floor, covering her with his body. Something sailed overhead, and she heard it tear through one of the displays. Glass shattered and fell to the floor, and Malachite held open his jacket to shield Danica from the shards.

For a few terrifying seconds, adrenaline buzzed in her ears, drowning out all other noises other than her pounding heart. She peeked past Malachite and saw security guards racing over. Outside the store along the mall walkways, the other shoppers were also plastered against the floor. One woman was sobbing, and everyone looked scared shitless.

Danica glanced into the main showroom and saw Alara covered by one of her bodyguards. It felt like an eternity had passed before the head of security said, "We've searched the perimeter and couldn't find the shooter.

There haven't been any other shots fired."

Danica was shaking when Malachite at last pulled her up. He kept a hand on her waist to keep her steady. "What the hell was that?" she breathed, her eyes darting about wildly.

Alara and her bodyguards, along with Suzie and the other employees, scurried into the room. "What happened?" Alara said, going instantly to Danica's side. "Are you all right?"

"I am," she said, trying to get a grip on her erratic breathing. "Thanks to him."

Alara at last looked at the lone ex-Alpha, and her gaze instantly cooled. "Malachite," she said with chilled civility. "What brings you here?"

"I was bored and heard there was a nice mall here," he said without missing a beat.

"I see," Alara said in a tone that suggested she didn't buy that line for one second. "And you just so happened to be standing here to save Danica."

"Lucky for her," Malachite countered, challenging her to say otherwise.

"What was that all about, anyway?" Danica said, looking around. "Was someone trying to shoot at *me*? Or Malachite?"

Malachite, frowning, let go of her and walked toward the display. He pulled something from the wreckage. His mouth pressed into a line to contain his groan as his skin began to smoke. "Son of a bitch," he breathed. "They packed a lot of silver into this one. It must be nearly solid." He held up the offending object and then sat it on the glass countertop.

Danica's heart sank. "A silver bullet," she whispered. "But why? Was someone trying to kill you?"

"Not me," he murmured, meeting her eyes gravely. "You. I saw a red dot appear over your heart right before the gun went off."

Everyone turned and looked at Danica. She gaped at all of them. "Me?" She pressed a hand to her chest in shock. It wore off about five seconds later as her anger exploded. "Oh, come on! Isn't it enough someone tried killing me once before?"

"Someone tried killing you?" Malachite asked at once, his eyes narrowing. "Who?"

Danica sighed and wearily rubbed her temples to assuage the growing headache. "It's a long story."

"Which we don't have time for," Alara said sharply, cutting into their conversation. "We shouldn't stay here in case there are more shooters. If you were the target, we need to get you out of here immediately."

"I'll accompany you," Malachite said, following them as Alara led Danica back toward the dressing rooms to change.

"Uh, whoa there, cowboy," Danica said, halting and holding up a hand in a "stop" gesture. "There's no need to ride along with us—"

"Actually, that's not such a bad idea," Alara said thoughtfully.

Danica's head whipped around. She gave Alara a WTF look.

It never fazed the werewolf princess. "He *did* save your

life. It would seem he has an inclination toward protecting you. A plus, in my book, as you are apparently in need of more protection than I thought."

Danica gritted her teeth and turned to Malachite. "Um, can you excuse us for a minute?" She grabbed Alara's arm and yanked her to the side. "Are you crazy?" she hissed under her breath. "That's my mate's sworn enemy! The Jafar to his Aladdin!"

"And I understand and respect that," Alara said carefully. "But you have to admit, he was an Alpha and a highly skilled fighter at that. He would be handy to have in case we run into trouble along the road."

Danica felt miserable. She couldn't blame Alara for playing Devil's advocate. Being the head of a supernatural race, sort of, she'd probably had to keep a level head about things. But if Gage found out she'd accepted help from his worst enemy and tormentor... "angry" would not begin to cover how he'd be.

"Besides," Alara added after Danica didn't speak right away, "we're heading in the same direction. Might as well at least let him follow us."

Danica gave Alara a pleading look. "Please don't make me choose."

"Fine." Alara smiled. "Then I will, and you can send Gage to me when he flips out." Without giving Danica another chance to talk, she wheeled about and approached Malachite. Danica rolled her eyes as the two began talking, and she ducked inside her dressing room. She wanted nothing more than to hide behind the curtain and never come out, but she also wanted to get the hell out of here.

Getting shot at was a great way to spook a girl.

The DPI, along with the regular police department, was quick to the scene. Danica was about ready to scream by the time they finally made it around to her and her companions for questioning. They said they'd let them know if anything came up.

*Sure. Like next year, maybe,* Danica thought sourly. *You guys were sooooo helpful the last go-around.*

After Alara snagged a shaken Suzie and asked her to check out their purchases, their company slipped out a quiet side entrance. Malachite had offered to carry their bags, but the women politely refused. Well, Alara had politely refused. Danica had more or less glared at him and mumbled that she could carry them herself. No way was he going to get cozy with her, no sir.

Truthfully, she wouldn't have minded if he carried the bags. The two she carried, in addition to the garment bag containing her dress, were pretty heavy; one bag contained a pair of fancy silk gloves, sky-high heels, a silk shawl to cover her missing tattoos, dangly earrings, and a sparkly bracelet. The other contained two sets of matching lingerie Danica had fallen in love with while she had been so elegantly plastered to the carpet. She couldn't wait to show the lingerie off to Gage. Despite the fact she really did adore them, she thought Gage could use a distraction. Hell, so could she after all this.

A few security guards of the supernatural kind flanked them since Alara was werewolf royalty and, technically, so was Danica. Malachite walked alongside her. When his hand brushed hers, she quickly snatched it up and crossed her arms.

He chuckled, and she resisted the urge to stick her tongue out at him.

Danica was filled with relief to find out Malachite wasn't riding with them but simply following them in case anything happened. The ride back was tense and mostly silent.

Alara sat beside Danica in the backseat while one of the bodyguards drove. "Do you have any idea who might be after you?"

Danica shook her head. "I don't know. I thought the whole debacle about the Nightshade Pack was over, but maybe Norman was lying. Maybe he's actually more involved than we thought. I just don't know what they could gain by killing me now. I'm already mated to Gage…." Her voice lifted on the end as doubt plagued her. She stared forlornly at her hand and where her Mark had been.

Alara took her hand and squeezed. "You're still mated to him. I'm sure of it. There's a perfectly logical explanation for this."

Danica appreciated the attempt at making her feel better, even though it killed her inside to not have any answers.

Every time she thought about not being mated to Gage, she wanted to cry. She decided to switch topics back to the shooting. The two exchanged theories, raking their brains for any clues as to what happened before the shooting or if they had noticed anyone suspicious, but they couldn't come up with much. It was frustrating. And scary.

Danica's heart sank. First, her mating marks disappear,

and now someone was trying to kill her. Why couldn't people just leave her the hell alone?

*Never a dull moment, right? Isn't that what you wanted?*

She wanted excitement, yes, but nothing on this grand of a scale. She was thinking more like moonlit walks along her mate's own private island. Something tamer and more romantic.

*So much for that.*

They pulled up to the castle in record time. Malachite escorted them inside, and guards met them as soon as they were on the stairs. Apparently, word had spread about the shooting.

"Danica!"

"Gage!" she called back as her mate broke through the crowd gathered in the foyer. He ran to her, and she wrapped her arms around him. He held her tightly as she buried her face into his chest, relishing the smell of him. Her senses were so much sharper now, and no matter where she was, she'd never forget his scent.

Pine, grass…. The scent of home.

"Are you okay?" Gage asked quietly, looking her over. "We were in the meeting when someone interrupted and told us what happened. Nik mentioned Alara was looking for an excuse to shop and figured she might try to coerce you into going with her."

"I'm fine," Danica said, giving him an encouraging smile. He already had so much to worry over. She didn't want to be the cause of gray hair sprouting up on her mate's handsome head.

Gage's eyes lifted from hers to gaze past her shoulder.

They immediately hardened, and he slipped a protective arm around her waist, pulling her close.

Confused, Danica looked over her shoulder to find Malachite standing there, staring evenly at Gage.

Lengthy silence ensued as the two men stared down one another. Gage was the first to speak. "I heard you were at the site of the shooting."

"It's a good thing I was," Malachite replied smoothly. "Otherwise, you might not be holding her right now."

Gage's grip only tightened around her. His fingertips dug into her arm.

Malachite waited and grinned. "Well? Aren't you going to thank me?"

A warning growl rumbled in Gage's throat. With a grunt, he gave Malachite a curt nod and promptly wheeled Danica about and up the stairs toward their room.

Gage kept his arm around her waist the whole time, guiding her. "Good God," he said, taking her bags. "Is there no such thing as a gentleman anymore?"

Danica let him take the purchases, deciding not to bring up the fact Malachite was the only man who'd offered to carry her things.

Gage carted her bags with one arm while holding onto her shoulders with his free hand. Tension radiated off Gage as they walked. She didn't need their mating bond to feel that he was about ready to snap.

"Um… Gage?" she said gently.

He stared straight ahead, those gorgeous blue eyes of his dark and stormy.

*Maybe he didn't hear me.* "Gage?"

His jaw ticked, as if he were mulling something over.

He walked faster, speeding up so they were practically sprinting. "Gage," she said, startled as he dragged her along. "Slow down! What's gotten into you?"

He remained silent the rest of the way, staring straight ahead and keeping an iron grip around her shoulders.

Danica frowned, staring at him with worry. Had he snapped? Had seeing Malachite in person again so soon after their last confrontation finally pushed him over the edge?

When they came to a jarring halt in front of their bedroom door, Gage whipped out the key and opened it. He ushered her inside and slammed the door shut, locking it.

He pressed his hands against the door, his shoulders slumped forward and his head bowed. He let the bags drop to the floor.

Danica froze, unsure what to do. She didn't even care if the ridiculously overpriced dress got wrinkled. "Ga-Gage?" she whispered, gently touching his shoulder.

A beat of silence passed before his hands slowly dropped and he turned around.

She gasped.

The agony in his eyes made her chest twist.

She blinked in surprise and worry. "Gage, what's wrong?"

Silently, he snatched her hands.

She blinked several times as he crushed her to him, not showing any signs of letting go anytime soon. He lifted a hand and cupped the back of her head, tangling his fingers in her hair.

In Danica's experience, guys rarely admitted wanting to be held. Most of the time, she found it hard to tell what they were thinking.

But with Gage… words weren't needed. Earlier, she'd been scared out of her mind that she couldn't sense him. But when two people were so in tune to one another's needs, they didn't need a psychic bond to tell what the other craved.

"It's okay," she said softly, reaching up and hugging him back. He trembled slightly at her words as she trailed her nails in long, soothing strokes down his back.

She rested her cheek against his chest and closed her eyes, smiling as she listened to his heartbeat. "Nothing happened to me. I'm still here."

"But for how long?" he whispered back hoarsely.

She pulled away from him just far enough so she could look up into his eyes. The pain that had nearly crippled her when he had first turned around and saw the look on his face was still there.

Along with terror. All-consuming, paralyzing terror.

She cupped his cheek and leaned forward so her lips were over his. "Forever," she whispered.

He didn't move to kiss her. He was still staring at her as if she might disappear at any second.

"You can't be afraid of losing me," she said gently. "You'll worry yourself to death."

He chuckled half-heartedly. "Already done that, love."

She winced. "Sorry. I didn't mean to worry you."

"What do you have to apologize for? It's not like you intentionally placed your life in danger." He sighed hard and ran a hand through his disheveled hair. It looked like he'd been in the process of pulling at it before she'd shown up, and it only thickened her guilt at having added so much stress to his already heaping plate of worries.

He frowned and stared at the floor as that dark look from earlier returned to his eyes.

Danica cocked her head to the side. "What is it?"

Gage's jaw ticked as he walked over to the bed and sat down. He leaned forward and placed his elbows on his knees, steepling his fingers to form a resting place for his chin. "Malachite."

"Oh." Feeling awkward, she went and sat down beside him. "He's… weird," she finished lamely. She didn't really have a word to describe Malachite. "Surprising," maybe.

Or "creepy."

While she could appreciate him saving her, she couldn't help but get the shivers that he'd followed her to the mall. Although he'd denied stalking her, she was certain he had been lying. Still, there was a surprisingly charming side to him she hadn't expected. From all the horrific stories she'd gathered from the Moonstruck Pack, she'd painted Malachite to be this ruthless, ice-cold villain. Yet he had treated her with nothing but kindness. The thing that bugged her the most was that it didn't feel fake.

*It didn't feel fake with your old boyfriend, Seth, now either, did it? Yeah. You're an outstanding judge of character.*

She pressed her lips together. Okay, so people could wear masks and be deceiving. That was a lesson she'd learned over and over again, yet she still somehow hoped for the best in people.

"I'm sure seeing Malachite again is stirring up a lot of bad memories," Danica said quietly.

It took Gage a moment to respond. "Not only that," he admitted, "but he's been there for you when you needed protecting the most. And I haven't."

He wouldn't meet her gaze as she leaned forward, jaw agape. "What are you talking about? You've been super busy with all this king stuff! Hey, mister, look at me." She grabbed his arm and tugged. When that didn't work, she knelt down in front of him and cupped his face in her hands so he'd have to look at her. "Don't go beating yourself up for not being able to see the future." She smiled and pinched his nose. "Knucklehead."

He snorted, a glimmer of cheer sparking to life in his eyes. "I don't believe anyone's ever called me that."

"It's never too late to start," she said with a wink.

The happiness on his face didn't last long. Soon, his dark brows stooped downward once more as he began brooding all over again.

Danica sighed and stood up. She went over to the only two shopping bags she'd brought home from the mall. "Well, if words won't lift your spirits, I have something else that might be able to."

He raised a brow as she began rustling around in the girly, pink tissue paper and lifted up two lingerie sets.

Gage's eyes widened a little as she grinned and said in a sultry voice, "So, Mr. Johnson, which one shall I model for you first? The red lace or the black satin?"

"Hmmm…" Gage murmured as he stood. The growing bulge along the front of his pants nearly made her pant as he approached and gently pried the lingerie sets from her hands.

He promptly tossed them aside and took her into his arms.

"How about we see how good they look on the floor, along with the rest of your clothes?"

Danica had to agree: the clothes did look pretty damn good on the floor.

After an hour of intense love-making and cuddling, they took a quick shower together. The "quick" shower turned into another half-hour love romp against the soaking wet tiles, and after finally prying themselves apart long enough to actually get clean, they dried off and dressed.

"I think contacting Violet is a good idea," Gage said, bringing up one of their earlier conversations. He tugged on a light leather jacket.

Danica groaned as she slipped on a pair of ballet flats on loan from Alara. While their waistlines might be different, their shoe sizes weren't. Alara had brought her and Gage some clothes. "Yeah, and I get that," she said, "but didn't you hear what she said when we saw her? People are watching her. And I don't want to be responsible for getting her killed or worse." She shivered just thinking about some of the awful things she'd heard Black Magic could do. "Worst nightmare" didn't begin to cover it.

"Right now, we need fast answers in order to anticipate and head off another attempt on your life before it happens. I'm not going to repeat the same mistakes I made last time. Besides, I suspect there's a connection between our tattoos disappearing and this sudden assassination attempt. And since we know the witching mafia was involved last time, I'm assuming they are this go-around."

Danica sighed. Sometimes, there was just no reasoning with the man. Flattered as she was that he was willing to do whatever it took to protect her life, she hated the thought of spilling innocent blood. Sure, Violet had done some pretty terrible things, but come on, she'd been coerced! Danica probably would have caved, too, had she been in her shoes.

Gage went into the bathroom to brush his teeth, and Danica plopped down on the bed to wait for him. A knock came at the door.

Figuring it was probably Alara with some news on the attack, Danica eagerly hopped up and scurried to the door. When she opened it, she stared in surprise. "What are those?"

The delivery boy peeked around the gigantic vase of red roses he was holding to look at her. "Delivery for Ms. Danica," he said. His spaghetti arms shook as he tried holding up the vase.

He screwed up her name, pronouncing it "DAH-NIA-CA," but she felt sorry for him because it looked like he was about to keel over from hauling the plants up the stairs. Not bothering to correct him, she quickly thanked him and showed him where to put the flowers.

Once he'd left, she squealed with excitement and went to sniff the pretty roses. They were huge, a mixture of fully bloomed blossoms and petite rosebuds. She'd always wanted someone to send her flowers. Her eyes started to well up. Gosh, she was so darn sensitive.

She heard Gage turn off the sink and shut off the bathroom light. Ecstatic, she whirled around. "Thank you so much! They're beautiful!"

"What?" Looking confused, he glanced past her. "Where did *those* come from?"

The smile slid off her face. "What do you mean? Didn't you send them?"

He frowned. "They're not from me."

"Then who are they...?" Her voice trailed off as she looked back at the flowers. They didn't seem nearly as pretty as they did a minute ago, as if the sender diminished their beauty.

*No way.... Please don't be from him....*

Walking over to them, she searched the leaves until she found a tiny card stuck on a plastic fork. Plucking it off, she gulped and opened it.

*Something tells me you like flowers. See you at the gala tomorrow night.*

*—Yours, Malachite*

# CHAPTER ELEVEN

GAGE WASN'T SEEING RED BEFORE, BUT HE SURE AS HELL was now. And the color of those damnable roses wasn't helping.

His fists shook at his sides. *How* dare *he? How cocky can that bastard get?*

If this didn't qualify as throwing down the gauntlet, Gage didn't know what did.

Danica pursed her lips as she stared at the bouquet and glanced at Gage. "I'm… just going to throw these away," she said, taking them out of their vase and tossing them into the garbage. Though he could tell she was trying to hide it from the way she ducked her head, he knew getting rid of the flowers made her sad.

He choked up for a second in surprise. In an attempt to hide his discomfort, he ran a hand through his hair. "Did you, um, want to keep them?"

She sighed as she stared at the garbage can. "Of course

I don't want to keep them if they're from *him*! It's just that nobody has ever sent me flowers before, and I got kind of excited." She mumbled that last part as her voice got softer and softer. She stared at her shoes and wrung the hem of her shirt.

He blinked, feeling like an idiot. Of course he'd heard women liked to receive flowers. The she-wolves never cared for such things, so he'd never learned to think of something like that. A wave of guilt slammed into him. It didn't surprise him she loved flowers, considering the amount of time she spent outside. And sending flowers was such a simple, romantic gesture.

He felt bad for making her throw out something that brought her joy.

Sometimes, he thought he would never understand human women.

*But she's not human now. She's officially one of you.*

That brought him some satisfaction, but he realized she wasn't like normal she-wolves. She had been human first, and thus, he would have to take her more humanly desires into consideration when trying to make her happy.

It made him feel incredibly dense to only now come to that conclusion. She'd risen to the task of becoming Queen of the Moonstruck Pack quickly. Despite her reservations and fears, he'd begun to think of her as one of the pack from the way she acted.

"I'll get you flowers," he said. "I promise. But first, there's something I need to address with Malachite."

He started for the door when Danica grabbed his arm. "Don't! Just drop it."

Gage raised a brow. "Alpha's don't 'drop it.' It's a sign of weakness."

"I should think that knowing how to pick your battles is a sign of strength."

He stared at her. That didn't cross his mind. With wolves, it was always bite first and ask questions later.

"What happened to the vow against violence you took for your pack?" Danica went on. "Didn't you say that after everything you went through during Malachite's reign, more fighting was the last thing you wanted?"

That made him go perfectly still with shock. His mate was right. Didn't he, King of the Moonstruck Pack, make a vow to set an example for his people? What kind of example would he be setting if he constantly came to blows with Malachite?

"Don't let him turn you into something ugly, because it's not who you are. You might be an Alpha, but you're also Gage Johnson. And I know you're not a bloodthirsty person. You need to stand your ground when provoked because we both know that's exactly what he's doing. He's *provoking* you." She poked him in the chest for emphasis.

He was quiet while he digested all of this. "You're right," he admitted at last. "I can't seem to think straight when it comes to him. All I feel is anger."

"That's natural. It's only expected after what he did to you."

It was hard for him to admit this next part. "I'm not sure I'm strong enough to fight the urge to slaughter him, to cause him as much pain as he's caused me."

"Hey, you don't have to do this alone." She took his

hands and squeezed them. "We're in this together. If you stumble, I'll be here to catch you. That's what people who love each other do for one another."

Gage's heart ached with pride and admiration. His mate really was a strong woman, much stronger than the world gave her credit for.

Danica smiled and lightly kissed him on the lips. "Okay, how about this? Anytime you start to feel angry, think of me. Think about how much I believe in you."

*I believe in you.*

Gage slowly smiled back. "Okay."

Danica grinned with pride. "That's my man."

After that, Danica managed to convince him to stay for a while and relax. Since there weren't any meetings to attend and no one had disturbed them, they could simply lounge in one another's arms. It was a welcome reprieve from the busy lives they'd led since mating.

Around ten o'clock that night, Danica dozed off. Though fatigue tried to pull Gage under, a restlessness hummed under his skin. Sometimes he couldn't shut off his mind.

His thoughts wandered to the political fight for High King. It had only been a day, but already the race had taken a deadly turn. One of the candidates had abruptly resigned and fled back home with his mate, who had been pale as a sheet. Later that day, one of the maids who'd been sent to clean his guest room had screamed. The walls had been covered in blood, and furniture was strewn everywhere, like a battle had taken place. Gage hadn't heard any fighting, but then again, he'd been busy. With Alara gone and Nik not any chummier with the palace guards than he was, Gage had no idea what was going on. All he knew was something violent had happened in that room, and it had scared the hell out of an Alpha who was known not to frighten easily. Gage hadn't told Danica for fear of her freaking out over it and demanding he pull out of the race.

He couldn't back down, not now. He was already in too deep.

Speaking of the race, there was also the matter of what he'd do with his Moonstruck Pack if he actually won the crown. Worries about how to best deal with Malachite's advances and protect Danica from harm gnawed at the edge of his brain.

That last thought also brought on an onslaught of guilt. He hadn't been there to protect Danica when she'd needed him most, and it killed him. *Damn*, he wished he had a journal to write in. Ever since he was little, he'd found it easier to sort through his feelings when he could write them down. For some reason, it made his problems easier to figure out, like solving a word problem in the grade school math classes he'd loathed.

He'd scoured the room earlier and found no paper anywhere. And since his mate was asleep, he had to settle for the next best thing.

He needed to talk to his brother.

Nik had always listened to him. Ever since Gage was a little kid, Nik had been there to guide him. He was a beacon in many dark nights of Gage's life. Maybe it was because they were close in age, but Gage had always found it easier to relate to Nik than his oldest brother, Elijah.

Thinking about Elijah brought on a fresh sting of worry and the heaviest guilt of all. Truth be told, Elijah was never far from Gage's thoughts. No matter how many bad things had happened between them over the years, siblings could never seem to completely forget about one another.

When Elijah had vanished and Gage or Nik never heard from him again, they'd assumed the worst.

Gage still hoped someday his eldest brother would walk back into his life, but he knew there was a slim chance of that actually happening. He'd never been that lucky in life to begin with.

He glanced at his mate. Except when it came to *her*, but he couldn't even have a normal relationship with her due to their circumstances. Sometimes, it felt like the world was out to get him. It was a paranoid way of thinking, but hell, most couples their age would be starting a family right now, not fearing for their lives because some psychopath was trying to kill them.

He sighed, then bit his lip to stifle the sound. Luckily, Danica slept like the dead. Gage delicately brushed back a strand of hair that had fallen across her face. She looked so beautiful and peaceful.

And so vulnerable.

Feeling a lump of anxiety in his throat, he gingerly untangled himself from Danica's arms and stood. Casting one last look at his mate and vowing not to be gone long, he quietly shut the door behind him. He wasn't surprised to find six guards outside their doors. With his wolf hearing, he'd heard them come by earlier.

"No one enters," Gage said, and they all nodded.

Still feeling nervous about leaving her alone, Gage forced himself to walk down the hall toward Nik and Alara's quarters.

The hallways were quiet tonight. In addition to the candidate who had resigned, one other candidate had been sent home immediately after his panel. It must have gone poorly indeed to warrant that kind of dismissal. There were three candidates left. The Council seemed to be pressing for a quick coronation so as not to leave the werewolf nation without a leader for too long.

The air in the castle seemed... *thicker*, somehow. It seemed the tighter the race for king, the thicker the tension in the air. Though werewolf politics didn't carry all the glamour of a human political race with TV ads, televised debates, and fundraising parties, they were just as intense.

More guards waited outside the rooms his brother shared with his new mate. Recognizing Gage, they let him walk up to the door and knock.

"Come in," called a feminine voice he knew to be Alara's.

Gage grabbed the latch and gently pushed open the door.

Their suite was actually Alara's room, so it was fairly girly for Nik. Mirrors set in extravagant silver frames lined the walls, along with a plethora of lilacs and white lilies. The four-poster bed had a white gauze canopy that flowed over the sides of the silk, lilac-colored comforter. All the furniture was white with silver accents.

Gage couldn't resist giving Nik a hard time about it the first time he had seen the room.

Alara sat on the cushioned window seat on the other side of the room, right in front of the huge bay window that overlooked the gardens below. She looked like a normal woman, wearing jeans, a simple purple blouse, and black ballet flats. Probably the most surprising find of all was that her hair was pulled up into a ponytail. Her legs were drawn up, and an open book sat on her lap. He'd never seen her looking so casual.

"No dress today?" he said lightly, smiling.

She smiled back and closed the book. "Nah. Decided against it."

He raised a brow. She never said something like "Nah" either. *Nik must be rubbing off on her already. Speaking of….* "Have you seen Nik?" he asked, looking around and noticing his brother was nowhere to be found.

"He went to go make some calls to try to find out some more information about the shooting. Apparently he has a contact in the DPI?"

Gage nodded. "Yes," was all he said. On the chance she didn't already know, he decided not to mention that said contact happened to be Nik's old lover.

Alara cocked her head and studied him with a twinkle in her eyes. "Something on your mind?"

"Um…." He shifted his weight and pushed his hands into his pants pockets. "I was—"

Alara rolled her eyes and smiled. She swung her legs

over the side of the window seat as she turned to face him and patted the now empty spot beside her. "You and Nik are so alike. Neither one of you wants to talk very easily."

"I believe that," Gage said wryly as he sat down. They sat in silence for a beat while he gathered his thoughts. He still didn't know Alara very well, but he trusted her because Nik did. And he desperately craved people to trust. They were a rarity in this world. "I feel… guilty."

"Why?"

"I don't know."

Alara pressed her lips together. "Is it because of Danica?"

Gage nodded.

Alara sat quietly for a few seconds. "I think I know how you feel. You feel guilty because you weren't there to protect her at the mall. And you feel bad for what happened to her before. Nik told me she was kidnapped."

Gage winced. "Yes. I should've been there to protect her then, too, but I wasn't. I keep screwing up." All his pent-up frustrations came pouring out. "I feel like if I don't watch her night and day, I'm going to lose her. But I know I can't do that either because she hates being babysat, and I don't want her to resent me."

Alara gazed at him with understanding. "Sometimes being in charge means a lot of people are going to depend on you. You're not always going to be around to defend the ones closest to your heart simply because as a king, you can't afford to focus on only a select few. You have to focus on the people as a whole and what's best for them."

Hearing those words only confirmed what Gage had

suspected earlier. The closer he drew to the crown, the farther away he felt himself drifting from Danica. Alara's advice didn't make him feel the least bit better. Instead, it felt like her words had cemented the weight on his chest.

"How do you do it?" he asked. "How do you watch over everyone and not lose your mind?"

"Oh, I've evolved and have grown eyes in the back of my head."

He looked at her then to find her smiling.

"I'm teasing," she said, poking him. "But in all seriousness, it's unrealistic to expect you to be everywhere at once. That's why you delegate."

"Delegate?"

"Yes. You have guards and advisers help those you love. That way, you can make sure everyone is always safe."

Gage frowned. From the weight of his expression, he knew he had his "brooding face" on as Nik called it. Delegating had always been hard for Gage. Truth was, there weren't that many people he trusted. He could count the number of people he had absolute faith in on one hand, which consisted of Nik, Alara, and Danica.

Alara cocked her head. "You look scared."

"I… don't trust many people," he admitted.

"I can't blame you," she replied without batting a lash. Ever since her family was murdered, he'd noticed a hardness in her eyes that had never left. He realized, more than anyone, she probably understood best how he was feeling since she was also an Alpha of sorts. "But trust me, you're going to need some friends in order to be a good ruler," she went on. "You can't do everything and be everything to everyone, and you can't be afraid to trust people. Not everyone's a Malachite."

He could argue that point, but he knew it would only make him sound paranoid and bitter. Sure, a shit-ton of people had let him down in his life. But had they always let him down because he never bothered getting close enough to them in order for them to find out his expectations?

*Everyone wears a mask....*

More like, he wore armor in the form of his cool demeanor. If he could keep people at a distance, they couldn't disappoint him. Yet, there was a part of him that yearned to trust someone, to find a few friends to share his burdens with.

He wasn't nearly as together as people thought he was. He was practically a walking contradiction.

Alara leaned forward, a slight smile on her lips. "It's okay to be imperfect and be afraid to trust people. I'm still working on it myself."

That reminded him. "Speaking of trusting people, do you still have that disc Violet gave you?"

"Sure. Why?"

He braced himself for rejection. "I thought we could use it to summon Violet and see if she knows who might have sent a shooter after Danica."

Alara tensed and took a deep breath. "Gage, I understand why you would think that, but this is the only way we have to contact her. We only get to use this disc once, and she's a valuable resource."

"Then why not use her? She gave us the disc for a reason. If this doesn't qualify as a damn good one, I don't know what does."

Alara stared at him, taken aback. She searched his eyes, deliberating. At last, she breathed, "Fine. I'll go get it." She went over to her dresser and pressed a button on the side that looked like one of the screws. A hidden drawer popped out, and she reached in and grabbed the disc. Gage wondered if Nik knew about her little treasure cove of secrets. Not that he planned on telling his brother anything. He certainly wouldn't want someone to spill his secrets. The fact she trusted him enough to get it out in front of him touched his heart.

Alara walked back to him and held up the disc. "What do you think will happen?"

"I don't know." He grabbed hold of the other end. "But I guess we'll find out."

"On three?"

He nodded and they held each other's eyes. "One."

"Two."

"Three," they said together.

The disc easily broke with a delicate *snap*. The lights in the room seemed to dim to the point that the room was almost completely submerged in darkness. Spooky white mist poured out of the broken pieces of the disc, coalescing in the middle to form a figure. The rough outline of Violet's body appeared.

Her wide eyes darted about the room, as if trying to get her bearings. "Hello?" she whispered. "Is anyone there?"

Gage and Alara looked at one another. "We summoned you here for a reason, Violet," Gage said.

Violet finally locked eyes with him, as if she hadn't

seen him before. Her mouth dropped open in horror. "You shouldn't have summoned me. Mistress will find out."

"But you told us to if we had to," Alara cut in, stepping forward. "We have something we need to ask you."

Violet shook her head, the terror growing in her eyes. "I can't do this. I can't do this, no, not now, not ever. She'll find out. Mistress will find out. She knows I left. Oh, God, what if she's watching now?"

Sensing they didn't have much time, Gage decided to be blunt. "Do you know anything about a recent hit placed on my mate?"

Violet blinked, as if startled out of her terror by his question. "Your mate?" she breathed, frowning. "No, they have no further use for her." She glanced over each shoulder and crouched. "Can't stay. Always watching," she muttered, over and over.

It might have been the shadows playing tricks with his eyes, but Gage could have sworn her fair skin looked bruised in places.

"Do you have any idea who might be after her?" Alara insisted, crouching with her. Gage decided to crouch, too, so he could be on eye-level with the distraught witch.

"No!" Violet shook her head, her long hair whipping from side to side. She looked like she hadn't combed it in a few days, and Gage could barely make out smudges of dirt on her face. What the hell had happened to the girl? She looked like a savage compared to the prim woman he'd met in the depths of the castle. "Please don't try to find me," she begged. "It was a mistake doing this. All a grave mistake."

She gasped and slapped both hands over her mouth as if to keep from screaming. Gage and Alara watched, both of them holding their breath as Violet began to tremble while tears poured down her face.

"Violet," Gage whispered, almost afraid to speak. "What's wrong?"

Barely able to move her head, Violet slowly craned her neck to look at him. He'd never seen anyone so terrified.

Violet leaned in, never blinking. Gage almost couldn't make out what she said.

"She's... coming...."

Her form was suddenly yanked backward, her mouth opening in a scream as the spell broke, and Violet vanished.

The lights flared back to their original brilliance. Gage and Alara sat there, staring at the empty space where Violet just was. Gage swallowed hard and fell back on his rear, rubbing his temples. "What the hell do you think that was?"

Alara shook her head, her face pale. "I don't know," she whispered.

# CHAPTER TWELVE

DANICA WOKE TO THE SOFT SOUND OF A DOOR BEING closed. As she blinked the sleep from her eyes, her vision focused on her mate, or rather, the haunted expression he had on his face. She immediately shot out of bed. "What is it?"

"Nothing," he muttered, running a hand over his face and smiling at her. She could tell he was trying to stave off her worry, that his smile was fake and only for her benefit. His eyes still looked cold, and her gut twisted.

"Did something happen?" she asked casually, trying to fish for information.

"No," he replied simply. "Everything is fine."

*Liar, liar, pants on fire.*

She continued trying to pry it out of him all evening and into the next day, but it was useless. Whatever it was he'd seen or done, he wasn't slipping up on it, and that worried her all the more. Normally, he'd tell her anything.

What did he feel the need to protect her from?

The harder she tried to push him, the more he seemed to close up. Because of more impromptu meetings with the Council, which resulted in one more elimination, Gage and Danica hadn't gotten to spend much time together the next day.

By the time the gala arrived that evening, Danica was ready to jump out of her skin. Any other time, she'd pounce at the chance to dress up and play princess. Yet as she walked through the dance floor in her red dress, with her arm elegantly draped around her mate's, she couldn't help but feel this was a waste of time. She had more important things to worry about, like what the hell had spooked Gage and whether or not they were still considered mated. She thought her not knowing what was bothering Gage only upset her so much because she *didn't* know. The bond was gone, a pill that was becoming harder and harder to swallow.

She kept hoping and praying it would just fix itself. Every time she woke up, the first thing she did was look for her tattoos. And every time she realized with a sinking sensation they weren't there, she felt her heart breaking all over again.

She felt her eyes tear up, but she firmly pushed them back. Considering the length of time it took to apply to her makeup, no way was she about to ruin it.

After making polite—dull—conversation with other royal werewolves, Gage pulled her to the dance floor. Light jazz music floated through the atmosphere, giving the gala a classy, relaxed feel. At least she didn't have to waltz. Tripping over her own two feet was the last thing she needed. Her aunt had teased her that she'd been born with two left feet.

She rested her cheek against Gage's chest as they gently swayed, feeling a wave of faint regret.

The decorations were beautiful and simple. White candles lined the room along with vases of red roses and black satin tablecloths. Along with the live jazz band in the corner, which had the members all decked out in tuxedos, the place had an Old World feel about it.

She'd always had a soft spot for jazz and had even taken swing dancing classes. Growing up, she'd imagined throwing a party much like this one at her wedding.

It made her sad to think that would never happen.

She'd never get to walk down the aisle in a pretty white dress, smiling broadly at the man she loved.

She'd never get to feel him place a ring on her finger or feel tears falling down her cheeks as she placed one on his.

She'd never hear "You may kiss the bride."

Her heart ached. She hadn't realized how much she'd wanted that wedding until the possibility of not having it became a reality.

"You okay?"

She blinked at Gage's voice, startled. "Yeah. Fine."

"You're not fine."

She pressed her lips together, the urge to spill the contents of her heart growing stronger. "I was just thinking," she said softly, "about how perfect this would have been at my wedding." She smiled. "But I know that's never going to happen because werewolves don't do weddings."

His grip around her tightened. "I know you've mentioned a wedding in passing, but whenever I asked you about it, you said it was no big deal."

She chuckled. "I didn't want to bother you with my silly, girly daydreams when you had so much on your mind. And then my Change was coming up and then our tattoos vanished…." She bit her lip sharply, wincing. She needed to feel some kind of pain as a distraction, otherwise she'd start crying if she thought about the missing tattoos too much.

Gage kissed her head. "Don't worry. We'll fix it."

"But what if it can't be fixed? What if this was all a big mistake—?"

"Don't say that," he said, grasping her arms and staring into her eyes. "Don't you ever say that. Since meeting you, I've felt more alive, like I know why I was put on this earth all along. I was put here to lead and to shepherd, but I wasn't strong enough. Until I met you." He smiled. "You always say I'm your rock, but in truth, you are mine. And I love you for it."

She smiled broadly. "Oh, Gage…."

He opened his mouth to speak when someone cleared their throat. They both looked up to find Malachite standing beside them. His hands were clasped behind his back as he smiled at them politely. His silver-blond hair was tied halfway back at the nape of his neck. His coloring was striking against the black tuxedo, and a red rosebud was pinned to his lapel.

Gage's hackles immediately raised as he glared at Malachite and stepped in front of Danica. "If you're hoping to cut in, you can forget about it."

"Actually," Malachite replied with that same irritating nonchalance, "I was going to inquire if Miss Danica received my gift?"

Danica saw Gage's hand form a fist. "I did," she replied quickly, placing her hand over Gage's and squeezing.

"And did you like them?" Malachite asked.

"You shouldn't have sent them."

Malachite shrugged in response, a devilish smile on his lips. Danica sensed that arrogant smirk only pissed Gage off more.

"Where do you get off sending my mate flowers?" Gage said in a low voice.

"I didn't realize she was your mate anymore," Malachite said, "considering she does not bear the Mark."

"That's beside the point."

"Actually, it is the point," Malachite said. "According to our laws, if a female werewolf is unmarked, that means another male werewolf can move in and stake his claim."

Gage froze. Danica's eyes darted between the two men. "Not this again. You said it wasn't true."

Malachite *tsked* at Gage. "Telling lies to her now, eh? You must be getting desperate." Malachite stepped forward, his cool eyes level with Gage's. "Why don't you just admit you're clinging to her because you know it's inevitable she'll be taken away from you?"

Gage's fist began to shake beneath Danica's hand.

Malachite never backed off. "There is a war brewing, Mr. Johnson. And you and I both know you won't be able to protect her when the time comes."

"What do you know?" Gage hissed. "What war?"

"What war indeed?" Malachite said with a teasing smile.

That did it.

"Gage!" Danica cried out as Gage jerked free of her grasp, aiming his fist squarely for Malachite's nose.

Danica held her breath, her eyes going wide as she grabbed for Gage's fist, but she wasn't fast enough. He was going to hit Malachite, right here in the ballroom in front of the very Council members who were considering crowning him king.

This would ruin his chances. They wouldn't crown someone who was prone to violence and flying off the handle.

And she was powerless to stop it.

At the last second, Malachite's hand whipped up in a blur of movement. There was the smack of flesh as Gage's fist connected with Malachite's palm.

He'd caught the punch, less than an inch from his face.

Danica's jaw dropped. *Son of a bitch.*

Malachite's eyes narrowed, the look on his face pure menace. "As I said," he growled, "you aren't strong enough to protect her."

Gage's eyes widened slightly. The people around them had stopped dancing to stare, and the maestro had cut off the jazz band.

Heavy, tense silence filled the room, amplifying Malachite's next words.

"I challenge you for the right to Danica."

# CHAPTER THIRTEEN

THE SILENCE WAS SO THICK, IT COULD BE CUT WITH A knife.

Danica's heart thrummed so loudly, she was certain everyone close by could hear it. They were werewolves, after all.

*Obnoxious werewolf hearing. I can't even be nervous in private!*

Gage's mouth flopped open in shock for a second before he came to his senses. "What the hell do you mean 'you challenge me?' You can't challenge someone for their mate!"

"Actually, he can."

They both turned to see Norman clad in a stylish black tuxedo that made him look like Gomez from *The Addams Family*. All that was missing was the mustache.

His seedy black eyes peered at Gage in triumph. "If the rumors I hear are true," he said, raising his voice so it could be heard throughout the grand room, "then I believe the lady is no longer mated to you. Am I correct?"

Gage's jaw ticked and Danica gulped.

Norman raised his brows. "So you don't deny it?"

Gage pressed his lips together in a thoughtful moment before speaking. "We don't know what has happened."

"Then your mating tattoos really are gone."

Danica clutched the shawl covering her bare shoulders tighter.

Gage's jaw ticked. "Yes."

"As is your bond to her?"

Every pair of eyes swiveled back to Danica and Gage. She felt the heat of their stares so intensely, she was afraid the flesh would melt right off her face.

Gage's voice sounded strained when he answered. "Yes."

"I can't hear you."

"It is," Gage barked, glaring at Norman.

Malachite stood by silently, watching all this unfold without so much as a hint of his true feelings in his expression.

Danica resisted the urge to growl.

*That son of a bitch. How can he be so smug during all of this? Doesn't he realize he's trying to wreck the one good thing that's ever happened to me?*

Of course he didn't. He was thinking only about himself.

"What the hell is your problem?" Danica yelled, coming up beside Gage.

"Danica," he said quietly, trying to grab her and hold

her back, but she brushed him off. She was so angry she could punch something. Her inner wolf growled at Malachite, who regarded her with that same coolness that had pissed her off to begin with.

"What do you hope to achieve by challenging Gage for me? I'll never love you."

"You don't know that," Malachite said.

"Yes, I do!" Danica pressed a finger to her chest, right over her heart. "Only I know what I am and am not capable of, and I'm telling you, there is no way in hell I could ever love someone who tries to control me!"

"I'm not controlling you."

"Aren't you, though, by trying to force me away from Gage? You're trying to bend me to your will. Well, I'm telling you right now that I've had about enough of that in my life, and I am sick and tired of being treated like *I don't matter*!"

Her voice had steadily risen to a scream throughout the tirade. Her angry words echoed off the walls, and she was breathing much harder at the end of her speech than when she had started.

Norman sniffed and turned his nose up at her. "Well, if you're done throwing your temper tantrum… which, by the way, is *so* befitting a queen."

Danica's face flamed. How dare he make fun of her! He was only trying to make her look bad in front of the other royal werewolves so it would make Gage look bad.

*Bastard.*

"As it appears you are no longer mated, I think the terms of the match should be declared," Norman continued.

"There isn't going to be a match," Gage said in a steely voice.

Norman scoffed. "I really don't think you have much choice in the matter. Where is Her Majesty?"

Danica blinked. Why was he bringing Alara into this?

The room looked around when Alara said, "I am here." Her voice was filled with power and authority, and it easily carried through the room. People bowed or curtsied as she strode toward them, with Nik following close behind. He wasn't wearing any of his piercings, and he looked downright handsome in a rugged kind of way.

Alara gazed at Norman coolly, though anger burned behind her eyes. "I'm glad you addressed me as I was already heading in this direction. What is the meaning of all this nonsense, Mr. Black?"

"It's not nonsense," he said matter-of-factly. "I simply wanted to ask your opinion on the matter."

"You mean Malachite challenging Gage for the right to Danica?" Alara said with a hint of sarcasm. "It's not possible."

"But in our laws, doesn't it state that an unmated she-wolf can be claimed by another male?"

Danica thought Alara would immediately rebuke that outrageous statement, but the princess went still and pressed her lips together. Danica's heart sped up.

"He's not serious, is he?" Danica asked.

Alara didn't answer. Her face went pale and she swallowed hard. "Yes," she said in a low voice, ducking her gaze away from Danica. "That is what our laws say."

Danica went cold with fear. "You can't—he can't—that's not possible! I'm mated!"

"Alas, my dear, your tattoos—or lack thereof—and your missing bond say otherwise," Norman said with mock sympathy.

Danica looked to Alara for help, but she wouldn't look at her. Gage's fists trembled by his side. His eyes were murderous as he stared at Norman and then Malachite, who remained completely calm.

"I don't care what our laws say," Gage snarled. "No one ever abides by that law now because it's archaic and barbaric."

"Makes no difference," Norman said with a sympathetic sigh. "The law is the law, even if it's an outdated one."

Gage growled as his eyes flared gold. "If it's a fight you want, then I sure as hell will give it to you."

"Gage!" Danica blurted.

Malachite grinned, looking every bit the part of the Big Bad Wolf he was. "I'm looking forward to our rematch, pup. I think you'll find I won't be so easily bested this time."

"We shall see," Gage snapped.

"Well, it's settled then!" Norman said gleefully, clapping his hands. "What say you to getting this pesky business over and done with? Shall we say the garden courtyard at midnight?"

Danica forgot how to breathe for a second. "But that's in an hour!"

"Look on the bright side, peaches," Norman said jovially. "At least you'll have it over with." He clapped her on the shoulder once before sauntering off.

Alara immediately walked up to them. "I'm so sorry," she said, her eyes begging them for forgiveness. Nik came up behind her and placed a reassuring hand on her shoulder. "I froze. I wasn't expecting him to spring that on me. No one has invoked that law in centuries."

"Is it true, what he said?" Danica asked, interrupting her. She felt like every fiber of her being hung on what Alara said.

Danica's heart sank when Alara at last turned her sorrowful gaze on her. She didn't need to hear her say it because she could already read the answer on her face.

"I see," she said, staggering backward. It felt like the time she'd missed the next bar on the monkey bars and had fallen flat on her back. The air had been knocked from her lungs, and she couldn't breathe for a few terrifying seconds.

She couldn't believe this. Was mating everything in this world? Did unmated female werewolves really get treated this way and just go along with it? Sure, Gage had implied that the werewolf society had "risen above" this law, but it didn't take away from the fact it was still implemented.

That notion was strong enough to encourage her hate, which was the only thing to break through her fear and shock at the current situation.

"It doesn't matter what the fucking rules say," Gage said in a low voice filled with rage. "I'm going to kick his ass, and that's all there is to it."

Without another word, Gage took her hand and pulled

her toward the doors. People parted as they passed, the chorus of their whispers filling Danica's ears. She wanted to scream at them to shut up, and when they snickered, it took every ounce of self-control in her to keep from tearing them to shreds.

Gage and she didn't speak the entire way to the room. His face remained hard and his jaw clenched as he practically dragged her from one hallway to the next. She knew that kind of rage-driven haze. Sometimes in a tough situation, anger was the only thing strong enough to get you through it. Anger at the world, anger at the mess you were in, anger at yourself....

She tried feeling angry, wanted to feel angry or latch onto an emotion that was stronger than fear. But all she could seem to do with every step was fall apart more and more on the inside.

All her worst fears came rushing back to her: the fear of ending up alone and with someone she did not love, the fear of finding herself in a loveless marriage she couldn't back out of....

Her knees shook as she bit back a sob of despair, nearly tripping as her legs turned to Jell-O.

Gage's grip tightened. "We're almost there. Just hold on a little longer. I need you to be strong, Danica."

She nodded. Strong. Right. What the hell had gotten into her? Where was that inner strength she'd so carefully nurtured while enduring all those years of hardship?

She suddenly felt selfish for falling apart when Gage needed her. Had she even stopped to consider what was going through his head?

He seemed to have it together so much that she often found herself relying on him more so than the other way around. But that wasn't how relationships were supposed to be. You had to lean on each other's strengths in times of individual weakness. That's what being in a relationship was all about. It meant you didn't have to navigate life's troubles alone.

They reached their room and Gage quietly shut the door behind them. In the tomblike silence of their bedroom suite, Danica's thoughts suddenly seemed that much louder.

*Will Malachite try to kill Gage to get the upper hand?*

*Does this mean I'll never get to see Gage again?*

Her heart nearly broke her sternum from beating so hard, and she found it hard to breathe despite her best efforts to calm down.

There was no calming down from this. Sometimes, you just needed to hold someone and be held.

"Gage?" she whispered, a tremble in her voice. She could tell by how hot her eyes were, and by how the room blurred every time she blinked, that there were tears in her eyes.

He turned to face her, his face scrunching up with worry when he saw her expression. He already looked so agonized, so torn. It was the same look she knew she wore.

She didn't need words to express what she wanted. It didn't matter they no longer had a bond. They didn't need one.

Slowly, she reached back and undid the zipper on her dress. As the silky material fell away from her body, Gage's eyes grew darker with lust.

She peeled the gloves off one at a time, letting them fall to the floor beside her dress. Next, she stepped out of her heels and pulled down the already soaked panties and panty hose.

With both hands, she unclasped her bra and removed it. Her nipples puckered at the sudden chill, throbbing because they longed to feel Gage's touch.

His gaze openly roved over her body as she removed the pins holding her hair in place. It spilled over her shoulders and chest in a cascade of golden curls. Removing her jewelry, she stood there and let him take in her naked body.

Her sex ached. Teasingly, she reached down and pressed the pads of her fingers against herself. She gasped at the sudden wave of heat her body responded with and began stroking the hyper-sensitive nub. It was so easy to get lost in her emotions right now. She eagerly let go of her worries, releasing herself to the sensations pulsing through her. Her breasts heaved up and down as her breathing grew more labored. She didn't want to think about tonight, or tomorrow, for that matter.

She only wanted to *feel*.

Gage watched without blinking as he tossed his jacket to the side and undid all the buttons on his shirt with expert precision.

Though he was undressing quickly, it felt like an eternity to her. She needed to feel him inside her before she came undone. It hadn't been that long since they'd had sex, but with the threat of separation looming over their heads, it seemed like she hadn't made love to him in forever.

The tips of her fingers reached inside of her, coating her in her own hot, sweet nectar.

Gage stepped out of his pants, shoes, and socks, and then yanked off his boxers. His erection jutted out proudly between his legs, the length of his swollen shaft making Danica restless. She hungered to feel him moving inside her, filling her up with deep, long strokes.

She probed deeper inside herself as he approached, his darkened gaze dropping to her hand. Silently, he lowered himself to the floor one knee at a time and gently pried her hand away. Grabbing her hips, he pulled her closer until her sex was touching his lips. He kissed her tenderly in sweet kisses that sent tendrils of pleasure curling up through her senses. She gasped, throwing her head back and leaning into him as he began to lick her. The sweetness of the gesture only made it more erotic. Not once did he become hurried or frenzied. No, he was taking his time and savoring her taste.

When she thought she would come undone, he rose and hoisted her up so her hips were even with his. She wrapped her legs around him as he walked them over to the bed, where they collapsed atop the soft silk sheets.

He kissed her on the mouth with the same sweetness he had shown her most sensitive area. The tang of her juices clung to his lips, mingling with their saliva as he gently nipped at her lower lip.

She opened her legs wider as he shifted his hip placement so the head of his cock nudged her wet seam. She ached deep within, her body longing for him to take her.

With a whimper, she dug her nails into his buttocks, urging him to get on with it.

He cupped her cheek, his eyes exploring her face intently. Then his mouth came down on hers hard, right about the same time he drove himself into her.

She gasped as he began thrusting fervently, and his tongue teased hers in desperate, breathless kisses. She bucked against him and ran her nails down his back. He groaned low in his throat, his strokes going deeper as he cradled her against him.

She clung to the man she loved as he drove himself deep inside of her, the dizzying sense of pleasure building in her core making her delirious.

Sex could just be sex, or it could actually be love given physical form.

As Gage made love to her, possibly for the last time, all the emotions of love and adoration she'd felt growing this past month came to a swell. She cried out about the same time he did, their hearts beating as one.

When she came down off the beautiful cloud of ecstasy, she sighed with contentment and relaxed against the sheets.

Gage, breathing heavily, kissed her on the mouth. "How was that?" he asked raggedly.

"Superb. As always."

He gave her a ghost of a smile, but the troubled look in his eyes returned and eclipsed whatever happiness she'd seen there.

He rolled over to lay on his back and wrapped his arm around her waist, pulling her against him. She clung to him as closely as possible and pressed her ear against his chest so she could hear his heartbeat. It was quite possibly her favorite sound.

A thoughtful minute passed while she traced patterns on his chest with her fingernail. She stared at the unmarked skin, feeling the calm of resignation settle over her.

And the bitterness of resentment.

"There's no backing out of this, is there?" she said in a resigned voice.

"No," Gage answered.

If it were possible, Danica would have gotten closer. She knew trying to convince him to run away with her was a moot point. They couldn't abandon their pack. She'd grown fond of them, and they really had started to feel like a family of sorts to her. Besides, no wolf who ran from a challenger would ever be able to call himself an Alpha.

Their relationship wasn't the only thing at stake—so was Gage's pride as an Alpha.

She frowned, wondering when someone would point out that he was technically "unmated" and no longer fit to be an Alpha. With all the fuss surrounding the decision of who would be the next High King, no one probably cared much about what happened to an insignificant "country pack."

Her frown deepened. The Council had to be aware of the tattoos' absence. Well, they sure as hell were now, thanks to the ballroom spectacle.

So why hadn't they taken Gage out of the running for High King?

Gage held her tight and kissed the top of her head.

"I will win you. You are mine, and I am yours, as it was always meant to be."

His tone sounded so reassuring.

But she couldn't help but notice the shadow of doubt hiding in his eyes.

# CHAPTER FOURTEEN

GAGE'S INNER WOLF COULDN'T WAIT TO BE UNLEASHED. Wolves, especially Alphas, took challenges of character very seriously.

And Malachite had thrown down an iron gauntlet.

Gage gripped Danica's hand as they rounded the corner of the last hedgerow before the courtyard.

The courtyard, much like the rest of the garden, was immaculately kept. Polished stone tiles arranged in a spiral shone under the wrought iron lampposts. It would have been romantic, had it not been filled to the brim with bloodthirsty werewolves.

Malachite stood at the opposite side of the circular courtyard, wearing nothing but a pair of sweatpants. Even his feet were bare.

His long hair hung freely about his massive chest. He was even more muscular than Gage remembered, looking like a striking mixture between a rock star and a pro wrestler.

Malachite's dark eyes lifted, and he flashed Gage a wicked smile. "I thought you had tucked tail and run, little pup."

"And miss another chance to kick your ass? I don't think so."

Malachite's smile hitched. "Careful, boy. It would be humiliating for you to boast so and then lose in front of all these royal werewolves."

"Who said anything about losing?"

Alara cleared her throat and stepped forward. She still wore her classy black evening gown. Most of the gathered werewolves still wore their ballroom attire, too. Gage heard muffled voices and could hear the scrape of money as it was exchanged.

They were placing bets on this fight. Not that it surprised him.

*Anything to make an extra buck... or an extra hundred....*

"This will not be a fight to the death," Alara declared. The steel in her voice said it was a nonnegotiable matter. Some of the werewolves growled in disgruntlement, including some of the women, but Alara went on.

"You must stay within the circle or you will be disqualified. The first wolf to knock out his opponent wins."

She gestured to each of them. "Gentlemen, if you would please."

Gage's heart sped up, not from fear but from adrenaline. He was, surprisingly, looking forward to this. He had been ever since he first saw his tormentor in the hallway and all those repressed feelings of anger broke past the box he kept them locked in and surged forward.

He wanted to shed Malachite's blood. The bastard deserved it after all he had put Gage and the rest of the Moonstruck Pack through.

Danica squeezed his hand and kissed him on the lips. "Kick his ass."

Gage grinned. "Planning on it."

Danica didn't beg him not to fight. Instead, she regally clasped her hands in front of her and stepped back so she was just outside the circle.

Gage couldn't be more proud of his mate, his queen.

She truly had changed a lot in only a short span of time. The unsure girl was gone, replaced by a woman with a backbone of iron.

Her strength fueled his resolve to win this for her.

He met Malachite in the middle of the courtyard.

Malachite cracked his knuckles and rolled his neck. "Ready for an ass-kicking?"

"I was about to ask you the same thing."

"It does not matter if you fight in your human or wolf forms," Alara said. She took a deep breath. "On three. One... two..."

Gage's heart beat so fiercely he could feel it in his ears. *Don't. Lose.*

"Three!"

Nik yanked her back as the two men burst out of their skins in a split second and changed into werewolves. Snarls and growls erupted as they lunged at each other.

Once the fight began, all Gage could focus on was the

enormous black wolf in front of him. He gave himself over to the majestic white werewolf he shared a soul with, giving in to its strength and its brutality.

He tasted the hot tang of blood along his tongue as his teeth sank into Malachite's flesh. Pain shot along his shoulder as the black wolf's jaws found purchase. It hurt like hell, but it did not disable him.

As they clawed and snapped at one another, spinning and rolling about the courtyard, all Gage could see was red. All sound leveled out into a drone that buzzed so loudly in his ears, he couldn't even hear his own heart beating anymore.

He could only see one face in his mind the entire time. *Danica.*

Thinking of her gave him renewed strength.

He had no idea how long they fought. He could tell when Malachite started to tire, and that's when he made his move. Malachite leapt at him, but he wasn't fast enough. Gage leapt out of the way and wrapped his jaws around Malachite's throat. If he could squeeze long enough and cut out Malachite's air supply, he could knock him out without killing him.

Malachite struggled, but barely. He knew as well as Gage did that with the way he held him, he could just as easily tear out his own throat on Gage's fangs.

There wasn't anything he could do. As Danica would have said, he was SOL.

*Gotcha.*

There was a weird shimmer of green light, and the fur began to melt away from the black wolf's flesh as it shrank and reformed into a man.

Malachite, completely naked, groaned and clutched at his head. His skin shimmered with thousands of green tendrils that crawled over him like worms.

Gage immediately let go. *What the hell is this? It looks like… Green Magic.*

Malachite continued to writhe on the stones, groaning while he clutched at his head.

"Look!" someone cried out. "Gage's paws!"

Gage looked down. His paws were shrouded in the same glowing green tendrils that slithered over Malachite.

His eyes widened. Freaked out, he immediately shifted back into a man and stared at his hands. The green glow slowly began to fade. He blinked. *What the—?*

Someone slammed into him, knocking him hard to the ground. The breastplate of a guard dug into Gage's bare back, the rim of the armor grinding against his spine. He gritted his teeth as two more guards latched onto him and held him against the stone. Gage managed to turn his head to the side so he could speak. The motion of talking was still awkward due to the fact his chin was pressed against the ground. "What the hell is this?" Gage demanded.

"He's a magic user!"

"Did you see his hands?"

"It was Green Magic! What if he's one of *them*?"

Whispers swirled around him. His inner wolf sensed the fear and shock of the people around him.

Wait a minute… they thought *he* was a warlock?

"It's not what you think!" he shouted. "I have no idea what happened!"

"Of course you don't," Norman crooned, stepping forward and smiling with artificial sympathy. "I've heard of warlocks not being able to control their powers in times of great duress. Then again, you could always be lying...."

Gage struggled as he fought to lunge at Norman. "You son of a bitch! You had something to do with this, didn't you?"

Norman held up his hands. "I'm not the one with glowing fingers. And magic never lies." He stood and turned to Alara, who had gone pale. She stared at Gage as if she didn't know him.

Her father, who had tried to kill her, had been a Green Warlock. Of course she'd be freaked out.

Someone had planned on that and was trying to frame Gage. But who? And why?

He glared at Malachite. Medics knelt next to him, checking his vitals. He was sitting up now.

And smirking at Gage.

Gage growled. The desire to rip the other werewolf's throat out shot to the front of his senses, nearly overriding his common sense.

"This man is obviously in possession of Green Magic," Norman declared to Alara. "As he has been caught cheating, that should disqualify him from the challenge, and he should be withdrawn from consideration for High King! He should be thrown in the dungeon!"

Alara snapped to her senses and glared at Norman. "We don't know what really happened."

"So are you saying you'll allow this potentially dangerous warlock to roam free about the palace? What if he is one of the members of the Order?"

"That's not true!" Gage snarled.

"Gage, shut up!" Nik barked.

Gage pressed his lips together. He got it. Really, he did. Much like how human law worked, anything he said could be held against him. And Norman had a reputation for twisting one's words around to his favor.

Alara's mouth formed a thin line as she deliberated. "Very well. Guards," she said weakly.

Gage wasn't surprised by her ruling. After all, she had the safety of the people around her to consider. She had to keep her personal feelings out of it. As an Alpha, he understood all too well the sacrifices that had to be made in order to rule.

Alara's eyes lifted to his, her expression heavy with guilt. Then her gaze hardened to cool steel as she addressed the guards. "If he's harmed, it will be your lives."

They exchanged a look and gulped. "Yes, ma'am," they said at once, fisting their hands over their hearts and bowing to her.

She looked to Gage again, regret shimmering in her eyes.

He gave her a small smile, letting her know he didn't blame her, and curtly nodded as the guards hauled him to his feet. They began leading him away when Danica shouted, "Get away from me!"

Gage's head shot around so fast that a nerve in his neck pinched. He winced, straining to see what was happening behind him.

Malachite, his hips covered by a loosely bound towel,

stood in front of Danica. She glared at him. "I'm not going anywhere with you!"

"I won you," he said simply.

"So? What the hell do I care? You cheated somehow, and I'm going to prove it!"

"Lower your voice," he said coldly, reaching for her. "You're making a scene. It is most unbecoming of a lady."

"How about this?" She raised her hand to slap him. Her reflexes were already much faster than they were before; she nearly had him when Malachite's hand shot up, and he caught her by the wrist.

The second their flesh connected, a familiar blue light shone on the back of Danica's hand.

Time stopped for Gage. *It can't be…. It's impossible….*

When the light dimmed, an indigo pattern of tangled Celtic knots lay on Danica's flesh. She stared at it, trembling and shaking her head. "No," she stammered. "This isn't right. How is this possible?"

"I told you," Malachite said, reaching up and taking a piece of her hair between his fingers. He ran his hand down her hair slowly, as if savoring the silky feel of it. "You were always meant to be mine."

Gage stared numbly at his mate, his entire being reeling from the shock. He felt himself go cold.

There was some mistake. Danica was already marked by *him*. She was *his* mate. The tattoos weren't there, but it didn't mean anything.

Did it?

Sensing he was about to snap, the guards started hauling him forward at a much faster pace than before. Gage regained a sliver of his self-control. "Danica," he rasped.

Her terrified eyes shot up and found his. "Gage!" she screamed. She rushed forward only to have Malachite snatch her up by the waist and hold her back. She reached for him. "GAGE!"

"Danica!" He struggled, straining to see the woman he so desperately loved but was afraid he had just lost forever.

The last thing he saw before he rounded the corner was an image he would never be able to get out of his head: The beautiful green eyes of his lost mate, staring at him as he was forced to abandon her to the clutches of a maniac.

And the triumph in Malachite's stone-cold eyes as he mouthed, "I win."

# CHAPTER FIFTEEN

THIS COULDN'T BE HAPPENING. DANICA REFUSED TO look at the Mark on her hand, though she could feel the magical residue of its imprint tickling her skin. It only made her more determined not to think about it, which in turn made her think about it. It was a vicious cycle of suckage.

After Gage was hauled off to the dungeons, Danica had begged Alara to let her see him. She could tell Alara felt guilty for allowing the match to take place anyway, and Danica would be lying if she said she hadn't played upon that guilt to needle Alara into allowing her to visit Gage.

She turned and marched in the direction they had taken him before the, "Yes," had fully cleared Alara's lips.

Alara had sent two guards to escort her, and Malachite made no move to stop her. Danica had almost wished he'd at least tried. Then she'd have another excuse to try to slap him.

163

She was so angry and confused, she wanted to beat his face in. She didn't fancy herself a violent person, but the idea of him touching her in the way Gage had during their mating ceremony made her gag.

She refused to think about that. Right now, she had to focus on being strong for Gage. Thinking of her mate made a deluge of sorrow wash through her, like the sun would never shine again.

Danica felt like an inmate walking Death Row as she descended the dank stairwell into the dungeons below the castle. Her knees shook, and she had to keep a hand along the wall to keep from tripping. The sense that her life was falling apart and all her dreams were shattering overwhelmed her. This couldn't be happening. Gage wasn't supposed to lose. He *couldn't* lose. He was strong and true and fearless and the man she truly loved.

Weren't the good guys supposed to win? Didn't that always happen in the movies? She suddenly felt childish for thinking so. The naive girl she was when she first met Gage was slowly slipping away, replaced by someone whose heart had stone walls built around it due to a lifetime of broken expectations. Still, the part of her that was hurting demanded an explanation.

*Why is this happening? Is it all another test? What good can come of this?*

She used to believe everything happened for a reason. "Tests are there to make you stronger," her aunt had told her when she was younger. It had been her response whenever something bad had happened.

It was "just a test" when her mom died.

It was "just a test" when her boyfriend dumped her.

It was "just a test" when she got made fun of in school for not having the most stylish clothing.

Danica had whole-heartedly believed her aunt while growing up. But with every new test she faced, and every year she grew older, she started to doubt her aunt's statements.

Were they all just "tests" or simply bouts of bad luck?

Danica was starting to feel like she couldn't see any way another test could help her. If anything, it was only making her more tired and bitter.

Torches lined the walls of the dark hallway at the foot of the stairwell. "This way, ma'am," one guard said solemnly as he led her through the passage.

Danica barely took notice of her surroundings. Shock came closest to what she felt, the same, familiar numbness that had swallowed her whole when she realized her aunt had abandoned her. The same way she'd felt when she found out her father was going to miss yet another birthday or Christmas because he'd be in jail again.

The dungeon was dark and well kept. She thankfully didn't see any rats as she'd been halfway expecting. Hollywood had ruined her expectations of what a classic castle dungeon looked like. This was the twenty-first century, not the sixteenth.

Each cell was about eight feet across and eight feet deep. Iron bars lined the walls, and each cell had a modest cot, along with a small sink and a toilet. Danica wrinkled her nose. Despite the modern accommodations in each cell, she would die if she had to do a number two in front of someone.

*With everything that's going on, this is what you're thinking about?*

"We're here."

Her heart nearly stopped beating as her head shot up. Werewolf eyesight, she had to admit, was pretty impressive. Strangely enough, of all the changes that had been happening to her body since she mated with Gage, seeing more clearly in the dark had been the easiest to adapt to.

She paused in front of the cell the guards had stopped at, making out the figure of her mate beyond the bars.

She instantly went forward and gripped the cold iron as Gage did the same. Their lips met in a passionate kiss, though the angle was awkward thanks to the barrier. The bars pressed into her face as she strained to kiss her mate. When they broke the kiss, Gage gripped her hands. "I didn't do it," he whispered. "I didn't use magic. I can't."

"I know. I believe you. Malachite had to have had something to do with it. He couldn't have been playing fair."

Footsteps approached, along with a deep voice that echoed off the lonely, spooky corridor. "Try to justify it all you want with your imaginative stories, but saying I cheated makes the outcome no less real."

Danica growled and whirled around, leveling every ounce of hatred in her body at Malachite. "What the hell are you doing here? Can you not even grant me a moment alone with my mate?"

"He is not your mate anymore," Malachite said calmly. "I am. I won you."

Her head nearly exploded in outrage. She was surprised smoke didn't start to seep out of her ears. "You—that—how dare you! I'm not some stuffed animal you won at the fair! Don't treat me like an object with no feelings and no freewill!"

"I apologize," he said, starting toward her. "I didn't mean to upset you."

"Too late for that," she snapped, smacking away his hand before it could caress her face. With anger fueling her resolve, she boldly walked up to him and looked him in the eyes. "What happened in the garden, or at any point after that, makes no difference to me. Even if you claim me as yours, I swear I will never stop looking for a way to break the spell."

Malachite sighed tiredly and looked at her with sadness in his eyes. "When will you learn I'm not going to hurt you?" He reached for her hand. She tried to jerk it out of his reach, but he grabbed hold of her anyway and held her hand to his heart. "I swear I will be good to you."

"I hate you," Danica spat, angry tears pricking her eyes. Dammit, why did she have to cry every time she was upset? "You have ruined the greatest thing that's ever happened to me, and I despise you for it."

Hurt flashed through his eyes, replaced by simmering anger. "You may feel that way now, but you won't always hate me. Either way, you mate with me tonight."

Danica could scream. She thought about punching him but kept her anger thinly in check. "Aren't you leaving?"

"I have something I wish to discuss with Gage,"

Malachite said. "In private."

Danica's eyes flashed to Gage with worry. "I'm not leaving."

"It's fine," Gage said, giving her a thin smile. "Alara promised she wouldn't let anything happen to me."

Danica smiled inside. That was a reminder to the guards standing nearby that if they broke the princess's commandment, they'd have hell to pay. Catching on, she said to the guards, "Well, you heard him, boys. And now you have a witness that Malachite was down here. And considering the princess is my sister-in-law, I'd be sure to make her proud."

Not ready to admit defeat, she couldn't bring herself to say "*was* my sister-in-law." She had no idea what this bogus Mark meant, if anything.

The guards nodded, each going for the gun on their belt. "We are loyal to our princess. We swear no harm will come to him."

Danica appraised them. "It'd better not." She brushed past Malachite, roughly bumping into him and causing him to take a step back as she went to the cell. "I'll find a way to get you out," she said to Gage. "I promise." She kissed him again as passionately as she could, knowing full well Malachite was watching.

He cleared his throat, a scowl on his face, which only made her drag out the kiss longer. At last she pulled away from Gage and shone a snarky smile at Malachite.

"That's the kind of kiss you'll never get from me," she said and turned on her heel to stalk off.

Gage couldn't take his eyes off Danica as she walked away. Even when his eyes started to burn, he didn't blink for fear it would be the last time he'd ever see her.

*Come on, Danny, look back at me. Please.* His soul yearned for it, more than oxygen or water. If he had a dying wish, it would be to see those beautiful green eyes of hers again.

Just when he thought she wouldn't look back, she paused with her hand on the wall and glanced over her shoulder at him. For a precious moment in time, their eyes met and he swore he felt connected to her. Her love shone through her gaze, so real he could feel it.

*I love you too, Danica. With all my heart and soul.*

And then she was gone, the tears shining in his eyes haunting him for the silent few seconds that followed her departure.

Malachite put his hands in his jeans pockets and leaned against the cell. He stared at the floor, a pensive look to his face. "I hated to do this to you. But I had to have her."

"Yeah. You sound sorry." Gage had to walk away from the bars. Otherwise, he ran the risk of reaching through them, grasping a handful of Malachite's freshly pressed shirt, and slamming his head against the bars.

The fantasy made him smile. Then Malachite spoke and things went to shit again.

"I can't wait to feel her body against mine as I claim her."

Gage nearly charged the bars. "You'll never lay a finger on her!" he snarled.

"It looks like that's not for you to decide." Malachite barely contained his smile. It looked like he was enjoying this far too much.

Probably was, that smug son of a bitch. Ever since Gage bested him for the rank of Alpha, he knew it was only a matter of time before Malachite sought revenge. No true Alpha could just walk away from a humiliating situation with his tail between his legs.

Gage stared at him with loathing. "You don't love her."

That caught him off guard. "I could."

"No, you won't. You don't know how to love. You never have."

"Stop it."

"Be a man and admit it, Malachite." Gage grasped the bars, leaning forward. "You just can't stand the thought of me being happy and getting what you can't ever have."

Malachite's eyes flashed gold as he snarled and shook the bars. The whole cell rattled as a low growl emanated from his chest.

Guns cocked behind him. "Step away from the cell, Malachite. Or we'll shoot."

The gold in Malachite's eyes faded away, and his growl turned into a dark chuckle. He smiled. "It hurts to be betrayed, doesn't it?" he said softly.

"I couldn't let you keep hurting people."

"And yet you hurt the only packmaster who would take you and your unruly brother in."

That almost hurt, had Gage not had years' worth of

horrific memories to dull the sting of regret.

"That's the thing about betrayal," Malachite said. "It has consequences. A single event can trigger ripples that set a plot for revenge into motion. As I told you when you beat me, Gage—what goes around truly does come around."

Malachite straightened and tugged at his shirt to get out the wrinkles. "I'm done here," he said to the guards. He cast Gage one last triumphant smile. "Think of me tonight when I'm ravishing Danica."

"Gaahhhhhhh!" Gage roared as Malachite sauntered away. The bars weren't completely sanded. Their rough texture grated against his hands as he pulled at them, but they wouldn't budge.

He seethed as Malachite began whistling.

*I'll kill you for this. Then you won't ever be able to hurt the ones I love again.*

# CHAPTER SIXTEEN

WITH EVERY PASSING MINUTE, GAGE WAS ON THE VERGE of tearing out his hair. According to his watch, which he kept glancing at every five seconds, thirty agonizing minutes had passed. Aside from the company of the two stoic guards who didn't seem particularly interested in him, Gage had largely been left alone with his thoughts.

And when you were close to going out of your mind with worry to begin with, that was a very dangerous thing.

One thought in particular kept racing through his head, and it made him sick at his stomach.

*That bastard better not touch her. If he hurts her, I swear—*

The guards who'd been watching over him slammed into the cell, making the bars rattle and causing Gage to nearly leap out of his skin. "Dammit! What the hell?"

"Sorry 'bout the scare, bro," Nik said as he knelt and retrieved the keys from one of the now unconscious guards' belts. "I was worried when I first crept down here that the guards would hear me. Luckily for me, you were pacing about and muttering to yourself like a lunatic. That created a nice diversion, by the way."

Gage was still trying to keep from swallowing his heart as Nik unlocked the cell and opened the door. "Thanks," Gage said breathlessly.

Nik grinned. "What are brothers for?"

"Does Alara know you're here?"

"I think she suspected where I was going when I said 'I need some air.'" He shrugged. "She hasn't stopped me. If anything, I think she wanted me to break you out."

Gage immediately started walking toward the exit when Nik grabbed hold of his arm.

"Whoa, hold up there, Prince Charming," Nik said. "You can't go barreling in there without some kind of a plan."

"I don't have time for a plan!" Gage hissed, trying to keep his voice down. "Malachite could be... fuck!" Dammit, he couldn't even bring himself to say it. He knew Danica would never willingly sleep with Malachite, which meant Malachite would have to use force….

*I'm going to kill him.*

Rage scorched his veins, making his inner wolf growl.

Nik rested a hand on his shoulder. The devilish gleam he'd gotten before every street fight and every werewolf brawl shone in his gaze now.

"Since you don't have time to make a plan," he said with a crafty smile, "it's a damn good thing I came up with one on the way down here."

Danica had almost made it out of her window when two men came in and grabbed her. She'd fought, kicking and screaming the entire way down the hallway as they dragged her toward her fate.

People stared and other royals turned their noses up at her, muttering about her "wild behavior."

Propriety be damned. She was not going down without a fight. She'd claw Malachite's eyes out if she had to.

She was still struggling as they opened the door to a large suite with similar furnishings to her own. Silk sheets had been folded back on the bed, and red rose petals were scattered in a path from the door to said bed. If this had been the room she shared with Gage, she would have thought it to be a bit cliché but sweet.

Now she'd be lucky if she could ever look at another rose and not feel nauseated.

Malachite, clad in nothing but a black bathrobe, stood by the fireplace. He turned and frowned as they brought her in.

Seeing him like that drove a spike of fear into her heart. She dug her heels in, causing one of the men to stumble. He growled and grabbed a handful of her hair, jerking her forward and nearly throwing her to the floor. She cried out as pain lit up her scalp.

It only lasted a second because Malachite was on the man like white on rice. His large fingers dug into the man's throat as he stood there gasping and wriggling to get free. "Touch her again like that," Malachite seethed, "and I'll have you skewered in your sleep. Now get out. Both of you."

He shoved the man backward, and they both turned and fled as fast as they could. Danica sat on the floor, trembling. God, she was so scared. Why couldn't she force herself to think straight?

A gentle hand touched her shoulder. "Are you hurt?"

She leapt back from Malachite's touch like she'd been electrocuted. "Get away from me!"

"Is that any way to speak with your mate?" he asked teasingly, remaining crouched on the floor.

"You are not my mate," she hissed, looking around for a weapon. It seemed Malachite had hidden anything that could possibly be useful in a fight. Of course he had. How else had he managed to maintain a choke hold over a pack of werewolves for so many years as an unmated Alpha? A stupid person wouldn't be able to pull that kind of thing off. He would have been assassinated ASAP.

Malachite's eyes hardened. "You can no longer deny me what is rightfully mine."

"I was never yours to begin with! Why the hell can't you see that?"

"Perhaps it is you who is blind. From the moment I saw you, I knew you were destined to be mine." He gestured to her hair. "Your coloring is so similar to hers. In fact, your similarities are so close, you could practically be her doppelgänger."

"What the hell are you talking about?"

His eyes grew haunted. "My wife…. She looked like you…."

Danica blinked. "Oh." She couldn't imagine this guy being married. "It's unusual to see a married werewolf," she said carefully, not wanting to rock the boat too much. He already had a few screws loose.

"Marriage still is an unusual custom in our world," he replied. "I married her when I was a human."

"You mean you weren't born this way?"

"Most of us aren't. I only got bitten the night a werewolf pack raided my farm and killed my family."

*Ouch.* "I'm sorry," she said lamely. That really did suck. No matter how bad you were, no one deserved to go through something like that. She'd lost just about everyone she'd loved under a rainbow of circumstances, but she could still relate.

"It was a long time ago," he murmured. His hand tightened into a fist. "I vowed to punish every werewolf I could find and make them suffer as I had suffered."

Danica went still. "All those atrocities against the Moonstruck Pack... you mean they were for revenge?"

Malachite's eyes hardened. "It was the Moonstruck Pack that killed my family."

Danica felt like she'd been slapped. All this time, she'd thought things were simply black and white. Malachite was pure evil and Gage and company were the good guys. Now, she saw so many shades of gray. Things weren't as starkly painted as she had originally thought. "Does Gage know?" she whispered, feeling shaken.

"No one knows... except you." He shook his head and looked at her. His gaze was foggy, like he was still trapped somewhere between yesterday and today. It was unnerving.

She tensed as he moved closer.

"But that's all behind me now," he said slowly, as if in a trance. "Now that I've found you again, I don't intend on ever letting you go."

*What the...?*

Danica swallowed hard and stood, backing up. "Um, Malachite—" Her back bumped into the wall. A table was on one side of her while the bed was on the other. Both potential exits were blocked. Damn, why hadn't she been more careful and paid attention to where she was going?

She blindly patted the wall, grasping for some kind of object she could use for a weapon. Malachite stood and approached her, blocking off her remaining exit. She could try to duck under him, but she'd already seen up close how fast he was. He'd probably capture her before she could make two steps.

He stared into her eyes and cupped her cheeks. The gesture was probably meant to be tender, but it was almost forceful. Danica couldn't look away; she could feel him squeezing her jaws, making them ache. "You're hurting me," she whispered.

He ignored her, the look in his eyes sending a chill straight through her soul. It was as if he wasn't seeing her at all, but rather someone else. "I can't afford to lose you again, Emily."

*Emily?*

Did he... did he just call her his dead wife's name? He did say she looked like her. Was the whole reason for his obsession with her because he was trying to somehow resurrect his dead wife?

She inhaled a breath. "Mala—"

His mouth came down hard on hers, stealing her breath away. She cried out in surprise as he kissed her fervently, the feel of his lips moving against hers foreign and unwelcome. Girls would love to be kissed like this, with this much passion and desire, but all Danica could think was, *No, no, no! You're not Gage! Get off me!*

She tried pressing against him, but he must have taken it as an invitation. He wrapped his arms around her, cupping the back of her head when she tried pulling her face away. She clawed at him, but he only growled low in his throat.

"I see you're as eager for me as I am for you," he breathed, his deep voice husky. "Very well. No sense in waiting any longer."

Her worst nightmares came to fruition as he began ripping off the belt of his bathrobe.

"No!" she screamed against his mouth, but he continued kissing her. He ran both hands over her body, tugging at the hem of her shirt while he tried pulling it up. Despite the fact she was fully clothed—ironically, in her "getaway attire," which consisted of a T-shirt and jeans— the intimate gesture felt violating.

Tears started running down her cheeks as her terror spiked.

He was going to take her, with or without her consent. If she managed to survive that emotionally, would she ever be able to get her life back together once the tattoo completed and they bonded for life?

A future with Malachite sounded too horrible to contemplate. He was too possessive, too deranged.

He wasn't Gage.

Could she shift in time to stop Malachite from claiming her? Would her wolf be any match against his and whatever powers he'd acquired to beat Gage?

His bathrobe was nearly off when shouts erupted from the hallway and the door literally flew off the hinges. Malachite shoved her against the wall, shielding her as the doors slammed into the opposite wall and splintered.

"What is the meaning of this?" Malachite roared, throwing her behind him. The bathrobe had fallen off in the flurry of movement, leaving him starkly naked.

Two wolves Danica had never been so glad to see in her life ran into the room. One had thick brown fur and was a bit worse for wear than the other. Fresh, red claw marks marred his muzzle, though they were rapidly sealing shut.

*Nik.*

The other wolf was solid white with eyes the color of a cloudless day. Danica's heart leapt at seeing her true mate, and her own inner wolf howled with longing.

"Gage!" she cried.

He barked in reply and then leveled his eyes on Malachite, who'd also begun to growl back. His eyes shone gold as his nails lengthened and curled into claws. His teeth had begun to elongate and sharpen, as well, making him look like a piranha when he smiled. "Eager for another whooping, pup?"

Gage's wolf snarled, the hair along his back spiked

and making him look twice as big.

Not giving Malachite time to change, the massive white wolf lunged forward, his open jaws angled for Malachite's throat.

# CHAPTER SEVENTEEN

I'S AMAZING HOW YOUR LIFE CAN BE GOING IN ONE direction one second, and then it suddenly changes in the blink of an eye.

Danica barely got a breath in before Malachite's flesh literally melted away, replaced by fur darker than midnight. His livid eyes lit up with golden hellfire, and he snarled, rising on his hind legs to tower over the other two werewolves.

He was big as a man and even larger as a werewolf. His teeth easily measured the length of Danica's forearm. His fur was rather beautiful, reflecting rainbow hues like oil would.

The brown and white wolves lunged at him. Nik went for his legs, latching onto his thigh, while Gage launched himself at Malachite's throat.

Malachite roared as Nik's teeth made contact. A double assault must have been too much for him to deflect at once. He focused on Gage, who would have had a near-perfect hit on Malachite's throat had the black wolf not knocked him to the side. Gage grunted, landing on his feet and charging again.

Malachite sank his claws into Nik's back. The brown wolf howled in pain, letting go long enough for Malachite to rip him off. Nik flew through the air, crashing against the wall.

Danica winced as she heard the crack of his skull as it slammed upside the stone fireplace. The wolf slumped down to the floor and slowly morphed back into an unconscious Nik.

A furious growl made the hairs on Danica's arms stand upright.

Gage slammed into Malachite's side, sending both werewolves tumbling toward the fireplace. They snarled as they grappled in a blur of fur, glinting claws, and sharp teeth. The smell of freshly spilled blood filled Danica's nostrils, and her heart leapt to her throat.

She had to do something. She was no longer the girl who stood by and let other people protect her.

She wasn't going to just let life happen to her anymore.

Summoning her inner wolf, she pulled the golden werewolf to the surface. She gritted her teeth to suppress her screams as her bones and muscles reshaped to turn into a creature three times as powerful as she was as a human.

Her senses sharpened, like someone had turned a dial in her brain. The wolf side of her growled, itching to spring into the action. And despite her fear, Danica trusted her inner wolf completely.

*I am strong. I am a force to be reckoned with.*

Shutting her humanity off, the golden wolf surged forward into the fray. The snarls and the sounds of snapping teeth that had frightened her as a human only fueled her with adrenaline as a wolf.

Malachite got the upper hand, rolling on top of Gage and pinning a paw against the white wolf's throat. Danica took her chance and pounced onto Malachite's back. She bit his shoulder, her paws scrambling for purchase as Malachite reared and bucked.

Danica's wolf took pleasure in the feel of Malachite's flesh tearing beneath her teeth. The thrill of the hunt excited her.

Furious, Malachite slammed her against the footboard of the bed. The blow was hard enough to dislodge her, and Malachite turned, his jaws opening around her throat.

He paused when he saw her eyes. The points of his fangs dug into her windpipe. All it would take was one good jerk to tear her throat out, and she'd be dead.

She stared back as confusion played across Malachite's eyes.

Through all the noise, Danica's ears pricked at hearing the click of a hammer being cocked on a gun. Malachite heard it too. His large wolf head whirled around, his eyes locking onto a lone guard standing near the doorway.

He was young, possibly still a teenager. His finger trembled along the trigger as he aimed the gun straight for Danica's chest.

She sucked in a breath right before the gun went off.

Everything moved in slow motion. She could see the bullet barreling toward her, its odd silver surface—

*Silver.*

Oh, God.

It was a silver bullet.

And it was aimed right for her heart.

She really was going to die this time.

Her heart stopped. So did her brain, because she couldn't move. Something shoved her out of the way and then a pained yowl came from beside her as the bullet struck home. Her paws slid against the wooden floors as she scrambled to stand upright and turn around.

Malachite's regal black wolf writhed against the floor as blood spurted from a wound close to his heart.

She shifted back into a human; the pain was nothing compared to the thought that she'd been about to die. She fell beside Malachite as Gage shifted back as well and knelt beside her.

Slowly, Malachite changed back into a man with a cry of pain.

Danica sat there, knowing the humane thing to do would be to comfort him. And yet she found herself unable to touch him. She couldn't forget what he'd almost done to her. Rape was unforgivable.

Danica couldn't speak. She stared at Malachite with a heavy weight pressed against her chest. "You saved my life."

Malachite stared back at her, trembling. "I had to."

"Why?"

"Because I couldn't lose you again."

*He still thinks I'm his wife reborn.* She didn't have the heart to correct him. It would have been cruel, considering the circumstances.

Gage squeezed Danica's shoulder and handed her a blanket to cover up with. "I'm going to see to Nik. And find a healer."

"No." Malachite caught Gage's wrist.

Gage stared down at his former Alpha with confusion.

"Please," Malachite begged, his voice hardly above a whisper, "just let me die."

Gage lingered for a moment and at last nodded. Not sensing any threat out of Malachite, he walked off to where a medic was treating Nik, who'd woken up with a nasty gash on his head.

Guards were pouring into the room. It wouldn't be long before the DPI arrived.

Danica looked back at Malachite to find him staring at something beside her, wearing the happiest smile she'd ever seen. His eyes glistened with tears. "Emily. You came for me."

*Emily?* Danica turned but found no one there.

Malachite reached toward the empty space, his hand shaking before it at last fell limp at his side. He sighed his last breath, his eyes closing as his head lolled to the side. His lips were still partially upturned in a smile, making it look like he was only sleeping.

Danica bowed her head and said a prayer for him. He had saved her life. She owed him that much.

Standing, she turned around to survey the chaos in

the rest of the room. Her eyes sought out the boy who'd tried to shoot her. She found him pinned against the wall by four guards, one of which was cuffing his hands behind his back.

Wrapping the blanket around herself, she walked toward them. "What's going on?"

The guards looked at each other, as if they weren't going to tell her.

Danica growled. "Look, I just got shot at, so I think that warrants an explanation."

One of the guards, a higher-ranking officer from what it looked like, stepped forward. "It's all right, boys." He was older, probably in his late fifties, with salt-and-pepper hair. He had crow's feet around his eyes, making it look like they were always twinkling. "Captain David Barrett," he said, bowing.

"Oh," Danica said, blinking in surprise. "So you're the man who replaced Gerard?"

"Yep. And just in time too. There's never a dull moment in this place." He sighed and scratched his head. "To answer your question, Ms. Johnson, we don't really know what's going on. All I can tell you is that this kid isn't one of my soldiers."

"What do you mean? He's an impostor?" He was wearing the same uniform as the castle guards, so she'd assumed he was part of their defenses.

"Sort of. He won't tell us who hired him and why. Or why he was using silver bullets." David studied her a moment. "You were shot at while at the mall with Princess Alara the other day, right?"

Danica nodded.

"Hmmm… that's too much to dismiss as a coincidence. I'd bet the same person hired both shooters."

Danica swallowed hard. "I don't understand why someone would want me dead."

"Your mate—well, I assume he's still your mate anyway—is running for High King, right? Well, everyone knows an unmated werewolf can't be an Alpha."

"You think one of the finalists is behind this and not the witch mafia?"

"I don't really see what the witch mafia has to gain from this. This sounds more like a werewolf is involved." He ran a hand over his face with another long sigh. It looked like he hadn't slept in days. Hell, he probably hadn't, considering the mess he'd stepped into when he took the position of captain. "I'm going to question the remaining finalist, Norman Black, myself. If he doesn't confess, I bet Princess Alara will press to hold a Trial of Light."

"Trial of Light?"

"Yeah. They're similar to human trials, except they use lie-detecting spells and other fancy things to make sure no one is lying. The attempted assassination of royalty, whether that be of a werewolf royal or that of some other race, is taken very seriously in the Underworld, and you are considered royalty. The phrase 'innocent until proven guilty' takes on a whole new meaning." He rubbed his chin. "Weren't you almost killed by a Nightshade wolf recently?"

Danica shivered. She had no desire to remember

those terrifying moments. "Yes," she whispered.

The captain's voice took on a chill that could rival the deepest winter. He bowed stiffly. "You'll have to excuse me, miss. There's a certain Nightshade Alpha I'd very much like to interrogate."

# CHAPTER EIGHTEEN

"**H**OW DO YOU PLEAD?"

Norman flashed the judge a jovial smile. "Innocent as a virgin, My Lords and Lady."

The courtroom wasn't as grand as the meeting room, but it was laid out in a similar style. The shape was circular, with raised rows of plush crimson seats, a section for the jury, the defense, and the prosecution, and a raised dais upon which sat three judges behind a row of podiums. The floors were made of a dark, polished wood that gleamed in the golden glow of the sconces lit around the entire circumference of the room. Crimson curtains hung from the walls, though they were there to provide color more than for practical use, since there were no windows in the room.

The courtroom was filled to the brim with royal werewolves, all of whom witnessed the garden courtyard battle. Norman sat on the witness stand in a fine, pinstriped gray suit with a red silk handkerchief fashionably situated in his coat pocket.

Several feet across from him sat Gage, along with his lawyer. If humans thought mortal law could be twisted and full of loopholes, it had nothing on supernatural laws. It took practicing paranormal lawyers nearly ten years of testing to obtain their licenses.

Megan, his lawyer, also happened to be a werewolf. She had a reputation for being a down-to-earth woman with a keen ear and eye for spotting the loopholes that often allowed criminals to literally get away with murder.

The three judges, which included a high-ranking witch, werewolf, and vampire, all looked at each other.

"Your blood test results revealed traces of Green Magic," the pale-faced vampire said, thumbing through the pages of lab work again.

"Apparently so," Norman said, raising his brows and shaking his head. "I was as surprised to learn that as you were."

"So you're saying you have no idea how you came into possession of Green Magic?"

"Not at all, Your Honors," Norman purred.

"And you do not deny you had Green Magic."

"Of course not." He shrugged. "I trust the lab work to be completely accurate. After all, you sent it to one of the finest labs in the country."

More murmuring between the judges. The witch glanced down at the glowing pink-and-purple ball on her podium. Due to their gifts at lie-detecting spells, there was always a witch present at every trial in the country. Some humans had secretly begun employing them too, though illegally. The paperwork to practice such magic in a human court was horrendous, not to mention all the spells the human had to undergo to ensure he or she would never speak of the Underworld to anyone.

The judges, at a loss, reluctantly let Norman return to his seat beside his lawyer.

So far, the lie-detecting spell hadn't gone off, meaning everyone who'd been questioned so far had been telling the truth.

Which worried Gage even more.

He sat beside Megan, who tapped her golden pen against her folder. Her eyes were narrowed on Norman and her magenta-colored lips were pursed.

"Does the prosecution have any further questions?" the witch asked, looking at Megan.

Megan sat down her pen and stood. "Yes, actually," she said in a dark, authoritative voice. She put on her hot pink, wire-rimmed glasses and smiled. "I call Norman Black back to the stand."

Norman's lawyer rolled his eyes, as if to say this was foolish, but Norman politely stood and sidled over to the stand. He lounged against the seat and crossed his long legs, smiling at Megan as she approached.

"Mr. Black," she said, "are you aware magic infection is extremely rare?"

"Of course," he said congenially, "but it does happen."

"And it just so happened to you."

Norman's lawyer shot out of his seat. "Objection! The prosecution is being antagonistic."

"Sustained," the witch said, with a warning glare to Megan. "Tone it down, counselor. And make your point."

"Yes," Norman drawled. "Where exactly are you going with this?"

"There's a particular type of antibody certain paranormal species produce that wards off magical infections. Werewolves are among these creatures," Megan went on. "It's estimated only 1 percent of the werewolf population carries this antibody."

"We've already had blood work done, counselor," Norman said with a yawn. "They didn't find this antibody."

"You're right. They didn't. Which means one of two things: Either you really don't have this antibody, or you paid someone to write a false report and alter the test results."

"Are you insinuating I sabotaged my own test?" Norman growled, his eyes glinting gold.

"I'm saying that for someone who was one of the final two candidates for High King, I wouldn't put anything past you. You may have started out with innocent enough intentions when you first decided to run for the crown, but I'd wager the closer you got to that much power, the more desperate you became."

"I did not tamper with my tests!" Norman snapped. "This is outrageous!"

"Then you won't mind if I bring in one of my vampire associates to retest you?"

Norman stalled. "I…" His eyes darted to his lawyer's, who minutely shook his head. Norman looked at Megan and raised his chin a bit. "You have no right to touch me."

"I have the right to ask questions when things seem fishy," she said with just as much steel. She rested her elbows on the stand and leaned forward as she lowered her voice. "Come on, Mr. Black. It's just one little prick. All we need is a drop. What are you so afraid of?"

"I'm not afraid of anything."

The lie-detecting orb flared to life, casting a pink-and-purple glow about the room every time it pulsed.

The judges' lips were weighed down by severe frowns. The witch snapped her fingers, and guards started forward toward the stand.

"What are you doing?" Norman demanded, his face going white as they seized him and forced his head back so his mouth faced the ceiling. "What are you doing!"

His lawyer stood. "Your Honors, please reconsider the truth serum. What if the orb is wrong?"

"That spell is never wrong," said the witch. "And you should know our laws by now, counselor. It is illegal for us to administer the truth serum without the person first activating the lie-detecting spell. Once it's triggered, he or she must consume the serum."

Norman thrashed as Alara walked forward with the serum, her eyes alight with dark satisfaction. Norman's eyes widened as she came into view, and she uncorked the delicate purple bottle.

"Bottoms up," she said softly.

The guards forced his mouth open, and she dumped the contents of the bottle down his throat.

He gagged, trying to spit it up, but the magic within the serum took hold fast. Norman quickly went still as a spooky white glow filled his eyes, blotting out his irises.

"Ask your questions again, counselor," the vampire instructed Megan.

Her expression never changed. Gage had never seen her wear anything other than her business face.

"Did you tamper with your blood test results?" Megan asked.

"No, I didn't," Norman said in a monotone voice. His tone was raspy, like the answers were literally being ripped from him. "I didn't have to. I infected myself with Green Magic."

Gasps went up around the courtroom.

"You infected *yourself*?" Megan asked, crossing her arms.

"Yes. I bought a vial of Green Magic from the Black Market and had a friend slip it in my food or drink so I wouldn't know exactly how or when I'd been infected."

Understanding dawned in Megan's eyes. "So you could truthfully say you didn't know how or when you'd been infected, thus avoiding setting off the lie-detecting spell. Very clever, Mr. Black." She shook her head in disbelief. "Why did you want Green Magic?"

"Because it was the cheapest."

Megan snorted.

"And so I would have the same abilities as a Green Warlock for a few days."

"Why?"

"So I could make it look like Gage Johnson was using Green Magic, and thus, eliminate him from the race for High King."

Gage smiled grimly. *Gotcha, you sneaky son of a bitch.*

Megan glanced at Danica thoughtfully, who sat in the row behind Gage. "Mr. Black," Megan said, "did you by any chance have anything to do with the attempted shooting of Danica Johnson at the mall? And at the castle a few days ago?"

"Yes. I hired both shooters."

Danica's lips pressed into a thin line.

"Why?" Megan pressed.

"To be assured Gage would be eliminated in case the Council, who already favored him, decided to still let him run. An unmated wolf cannot be an Alpha... or a High King."

"There's also an eye-witness account of you conducting a late-night meeting with Malachite."

"Yes."

"Tell us about that."

"I needed him."

Megan's jaw ticked when he didn't go on. "*Why*, Mr. Black?"

"Because I knew Malachite was infatuated with Danica, and I needed a reason to make him want to be near her all the time. I knew he would want to protect the woman who resembled his dead wife, thus pitting him against Gage."

"So Malachite was a distraction, I take it?"

An unexpected pang of pity over Malachite's death went through Gage. He had been played, just as Gage had. All so Norman could get closer to the crown.

Norman was exactly the kind of politician Gage

despised. He felt no regret in ruining the lives of people below him if it meant getting what he wanted.

"How did you get rid of the tattoos?" Megan said.

"I didn't get rid of them," Norman answered. "A witch I blackmailed cast a spell that hid the tattoos from sight and muted the bond between Danica and Gage."

"Is it permanent?"

"No. The spell will wear off on the next full moon."

"So they're still mated?"

"Yes."

Danica bit back a squeal and reached forward. Gage took her hand and squeezed, his smile as wide as hers.

Megan looked around. "Any further questions?" When no one nodded, Megan started to walk away and then paused. "Oh, I did have one more. Do you have any ties to the witch mafia or know anyone who does?"

"No."

Megan's shoulders fell. It was smart, digging for a lead while a criminal was under the influence of the truth serum. Too bad Norman didn't have any connections.

"No further questions," Megan said, walking back to Gage and rejoining him at their table.

Gage leaned into her. "You're too smart for your own good."

She shrugged, as if her stroke of genius had been nothing. "My gut still said he was hiding something. No one had phrased the questions in a way that would make him lie and allow the lie-detecting spell to pick up on it."

Gage reached over and squeezed her hand with gratitude. "Thank you."

"Don't mention it," she said with a wink and a foxy smile.

The witch snapped her fingers, and the glow faded from Norman's eyes. He shook his head and blinked several times, squinting at his surroundings. When his face landed on Alara, who stood beside him, he frowned. "What are you smirking for?"

"You were right, Mr. Black," Alara said, giving him a dark smile. "Magic never lies." She looked at the judges, who stood. Everyone else in the room rose.

"Norman Black of the Nightshade Pack, you are hereby stripped of your rank as Alpha and are sentenced to one hundred years in Vulcan," said the witch.

Gage trembled internally at hearing that prison's name. It was the one place in the Underworld where only the vilest of criminals were sent.

"You are also disqualified from running for High King," the witch went on. The gavel slammed down, the clank of wood against wood ringing throughout the room.

Everyone on Gage's side stood and cheered. Gage hugged Danica, laughing. He felt like the weight of the world had been lifted from his shoulders.

Another gavel slammed down, interrupting their impromptu celebration.

"We have just gotten in the results for High King," Alara announced. A hush fell over the room as everyone waited in anticipation.

Gage mostly felt confused. Everyone had been eliminated from the running. Since the fight with Malachite, and his subsequent disqualification, he hadn't been told he'd been allowed back into the competition.

Alara's eyes sparkled, and she could barely contain her smile. "It is both my honor and pleasure to announce that the Council has ruled that Gage Johnson will be the next High King."

The floor nearly dropped out from underneath Gage.

It couldn't be true. This had to be a cosmic joke.

But as the crowd gathered around him and other royals congratulated him, he knew this was real.

*High King.* He was actually going to be High King.

# CHAPTER NINETEEN

"SO THEY ULTIMATELY CHOSE GAGE AS THE HIGH King because they respected his ideals and his honor," Danica gushed to the three women preparing her for the impending coronation. "Once they learned what he did to save the Moonstruck Pack from Malachite, they knew he valued other people's well-being above his own. That's how they decided he'd make the best king."

"Wow," one said with raised eyebrows. "He sounds like an honorable man."

"Not to mention he's so much hotter than King Victor was," the teenager, Marie, breathed with a dreamy look on her face.

Danica giggled as the head maid swatted at Marie, frowning. Marie blushed and went back to work at adjusting the poufy skirts around Danica.

The dress was beautiful. The skirts were eggshell-colored silk, which bunched in pearl clusters. The long bell sleeves were white lace dotted with tiny diamonds that sparkled every time she moved, and the corset was patterned in gold and silver whorls and filigree. True to popular belief, the corset was uncomfortable and stiff, but Danica forgave those vices because of how awesome it made her boobs look.

A diamond choker encircled her neck, and two large diamond studs shone from her ears. Her hair had been curled into dozens of ringlets and left down to trail over her shoulders and back. A few tiny tendrils curled near her face, framing it. Her makeup was light; she wore only a thin layer of powder, mascara, and soft pink rouge that matched her lipstick. It was the kind of natural look she could never seem to pull off on her own.

Marie, while being a bit of a blabbermouth, sure knew her way around a makeup kit.

The whole situation seemed like a dream as they finished preparing her. It still hadn't fully hit Danica what was about to happen. The girls made light chatter as they wrapped up, and then they guided her to the cathedral where the coronation was to be held.

Dozens of rose vases sitting on white pedestals lined the hallway, alternating with golden candelabra. It was beautiful and romantic, though Danica thought it was a bit of an odd decoration choice for a coronation. Then again, what the hell did she know about these things? She'd never been crowned a queen before.

Holy shit, she was about to be crowned High Queen, in a freaking castle!

She almost started hyperventilating again.

"Just breathe," the eldest maid said. They were all wearing matching dresses of red taffeta that were feminine and tasteful.

They stopped before the massive oak doors that marked the entrance to the cathedral. Much like the rest of the castle, the doors had been carved with moons, wolves, and the outline of thousands of trees and roses. It made it look more ancient and powerful.

Two guards outfitted in red dress uniforms with golden brocade bowed to her at the doors. "Ready, Your Highness?"

A nervous thrill went through Danica. She was only beginning to get used to her packmates occasionally calling her "Your Highness" back in Moonstruck. Now the phrase took on a whole new meaning.

With a nod, she gulped and sucked in a tight breath as they pulled the doors open.

The room was huge. Rows of cherry wood pews stretched to the stage along either side of a long, red velvet carpet. Rose petals had been scattered along the walkway. More roses hung from the rafters, their blossom-studded vines forming graceful arcs throughout the rounded ceiling. Long, wooden beams stretched along the ceiling, and windows of stained glass lined the walls. More golden candelabra lit with glimmering white candles dotted the room.

The sheer beauty of it took Danica's breath away.

A large golden pipe organ stood against the back wall, its tiered pipes singing a familiar melody.

Danica blinked. Why on earth was it playing "Here

Comes the Bride?"

Then it hit her.

Her eyes darted about the room, taking in the decorations again.

This wasn't just a coronation—it was a wedding.

Danica let out a sob that was partially a laugh.

"Don't start crying!" the head maid hissed, dabbing at Danica's cheeks with a handkerchief. "You'll ruin your makeup before you even say 'I do!'"

"I just can't believe this," Danica blubbered through her tears. It was perfect, down to the last candlestick.

A dream wedding from a fairy tale, in her very own castle.

And at the end of the walkway stood her prince, no, her *king*, waiting for her with a smile on his face.

Gage looked stunning in a black uniform with golden brocade along the sleeves and a red satin sash that crossed his chest. A long cloak of red velvet outlined in white fur hung from his shoulders. He really did look like a prince out of a storybook.

One of her maids handed her a bouquet of red roses and urged her to walk. She slowly made her way down the aisle, fighting back the tears threatening to spill down her cheeks and streak her mascara.

Her heart swelled with love and joy as she met Gage at the stage and took his arm.

He beamed at her. "Is it everything you dreamed it would be?"

"I can't believe you did this for me," she said softly. "It's amazing. More than amazing. It's perfect."

Adoration and love shone in his eyes. "How's about we walk toward that happily-ever-after now?"

She grinned at him. "After you, my king."

And together, they ascended the steps leading up to the priest.

The ceremony was beautiful. Though the sheer number of people present had initially freaked Danica out, she found once the silver crown had been placed upon her head, she didn't fear them anymore. That crown made her feel powerful, more in control, like she could take on the world without regret.

Dancing in her king's—and new husband's—arms afterward had been even dreamier.

High up in the castle, in their gigantic private suite, Danica and Gage toasted one another. Danica still couldn't get over the shock of her new position in this world. Everything had happened so quickly she knew she'd be feeling whiplash for at least a week, if not longer.

She and Gage were dressed in nothing but bathrobes. A bottle of open champagne chilled in an ice bucket next to their bed. They toasted one another and sipped. "I wish they could've figured out a way to restore our tattoos," Danica said with a bit of sadness. "It's the only thing that would have made this night more perfect."

"Yeah," Gage sighed. "It's too bad they couldn't find the original witch who'd done it. It's as if she never existed, which supports my whole alias theory. Oh, well. There's nothing to be done for it. At least we'll get them back in a month's time."

Danica smiled. She couldn't wait. "Are Nik and Alara really leaving tomorrow morning?"

"Yes," Gage said, his eyes growing troubled. "Nik says he doesn't mind taking over as the new Alpha of the Moonstruck Pack, and that Alara doesn't have a problem with moving. I think she has enough bad memories of this place and needs to start over somewhere."

Danica waited. "But?" she asked gently.

Gage sighed. "But I know how reluctant Nik was to lead. I tried pushing the Alpha role on him sooner, but he would have no part of it."

"People change," Danica said simply. "Look at us. You didn't want to be High King, and now you're excited."

Gage's eyes sparkled. "It couldn't have worked out any better," he admitted. "I was afraid this position would put you in more danger, but now I see you couldn't be any better protected than where you are right now. And I have so many ideas I want to implement. I really think I can do our race some good."

Danica squeezed his hand. "And I'll be right here beside you." She sat her champagne flute down on the nightstand and rolled over onto her back with a sigh. "Now I just have to figure out what I want to do. I can't just sit idly by and do nothing with my power. I have to make good use of it."

"You'll think of something," Gage said, curling up beside her. A mischievous glimmer caught his eyes as he slowly smiled. "You know what jump-starts inspiration?"

"Hmmm?"

He nipped at her earlobe, his voice growing huskier. "Sex. Lots of hot, pre-honeymoon sex."

Danica felt her nipples pucker in anticipation. "I haven't heard that theory, but I'm willing to test it out."

She wrapped her arms around him as he began to undress her.

# CHAPTER TWENTY

DANICA SQUINTED AGAINST THE LATE AFTERNOON sunlight. It cascaded along the top of the forest below the cabin and silhouetted the mountain in the distance. The sky was a clear blue, gradually becoming more orange the closer you looked at the horizon.

She had never been to Boulder, Colorado, but she never wanted to leave. Up here in the mountains, among nature in Gage's private cabin, her old worries felt like they were a world away.

They'd been there for a week on their honeymoon, and it was everything she had imagined it would be. Lots of private time with Gage, most of which was spent having hot sex or lying in a tangle of limbs on their bed while cuddling and laughing; roaming the forest in their wolf forms, since he owned the property and hunters weren't allowed; no one trying to kill her or break them up....

You really learned to appreciate "the joy of life" after

someone tried to take yours away.

Feeling more relaxed and at peace than she had in years, she closed her eyes and inhaled the crisp, fresh air.

A familiar scent trailed toward her nose, and she leaned backward as Gage's arms wrapped around her.

"Hmmm," she murmured dreamily, tipping her head back to give him a kiss. "I could get used to this."

"Me too."

"Do we really have to leave tomorrow?"

He winced. "Afraid so."

She sighed and rested her head back against his chest. "I knew we'd have to go back to our lives eventually." She smiled. "I still can't believe we're royalty, like, *the* royalty."

"That makes two of us, love," he said, smiling back, although it looked forced.

She could sense his nervous energy, and she reached out to squeeze his arm. "Don't worry. I'll be right here beside you. We'll figure it out together."

His features relaxed. "I couldn't ask for a better queen. I can't wait to see you as a mother. You're going to be outstanding."

She whirled around. "Mother?"

"Yeah," he said with a devilish grin, leaning in to nuzzle her earlobe. "The way we've been going at it, I wouldn't be surprised if pups were on the way."

Her face flamed. Sure, it had crossed her mind she could become pregnant since they didn't use protection. But children—er, "pups"—were the furthest thing from her mind.

The thought of being a mother and creating a family

with Gage filled her with joy. Her eyes slicked with tears, and she smiled broadly. "That sounds wonderful," she whispered to him.

His eyes ducked to her lips and he bent his head to kiss her.

"Oh!" she said, putting a finger to his lips to stop him. "That reminds me." An excited sparkle filled her eyes. "I know what I want to use my newly given power for."

He raised his brows, smiling. "Oh?"

She nodded firmly. She'd never been so sure of anything in her life, other than mating with Gage. "I'm going to abolish that vile law about unmated she-wolves. I want to be an advocate for she-wolf rights. And not just she-wolves, but any creature that's unfairly treated. It just isn't right, and dammit, I'm not going to stand by when I can do something about it!"

She barely got the last words out when Gage leaned forward and kissed her passionately. "I'm so proud of you," he said, cupping her face in his hands.

She beamed at him.

He started to kiss her again when his cell phone went off.

Danica broke off to say, "Shouldn't you get that? It could be important."

"If it is, they'll leave a message or call back." He enslaved her mouth once more.

The phone finally stopped ringing only to start up again a few seconds later.

And again a third and fourth time.

Finally, Gage pulled away with a growl and said, "I

can't even enjoy my damn honeymoon without interruption?" He stalked over to the phone and frowned.

Danica came up beside him and peered over his shoulder to look at the Caller ID. "Unknown," she murmured, looking at him in question.

He shrugged and pressed talk. "Who is this?"

Danica could hear a woman speaking on the other end. "Um, Gage? Gage Johnson?"

"Yes?" he said tersely.

"Um, sorry to bother you. Is this a bad time?"

"Yes," he said slowly, but he didn't elaborate. "Who is this?"

"Oh, jeez." The sound of flesh hitting flesh, like someone smacked their palm against their forehead, came through the other line. "I'm sorry. I forgot I'm borrowing a phone. This is Verika Tate."

*Verika, Verika....* Danica remembered that name. Wasn't she the ex-girlfriend of Nik's who joined the DPI as a field agent? What was she doing blowing up Gage's phone?

Gage blinked in surprise. "I didn't recognize your voice," he said, his tone noticeably softer. "Sorry for being short with you. What's wrong?"

Silence met his question. "Verika?" he asked.

"Yes, yes, I'm still here. Sorry." She took a deep breath and let it out. "Gosh, I don't know where to begin."

"Just start at the beginning," Gage said calmly.

"Um… we've apprehended someone tied to the witch mafia. We believe he has a direct link to Mistress Black."

They both leaned into the phone, their spines

straightening. "And?" Gage asked eagerly. "Did you find out anything?"

"He won't talk. And I'm hesitant to use… other methods of persuasion on him."

"Why on earth not? If he's responsible in any way for the deaths of all those people—"

"He's your brother!" Verika blurted.

Gage's words dried up and he went perfectly still.

Danica froze, unsure what to say.

When Gage finally recovered, he blinked and shouted, "*Nik is in jail*?"

"Easy on the yelling, big boy," Verika said gently. "And no, of course it's not Nik. I meant your *other* brother."

"I have no other…." Gage's voice trailed off as a haunted look came over his eyes. "No," he whispered. "It can't be. He's dead."

"Well, I'm looking at him right now, and he seems very much alive to me."

Gage gripped the cell phone so hard, Danica was afraid he might break it. She reached up to steady him. "Gage?" she asked softly.

Gage's grip faltered, and he nearly dropped the phone. Slowly, he looked at Danica, his eyes wide.

"It's my eldest brother, Elijah. He's alive."

## END OF BOOK 3

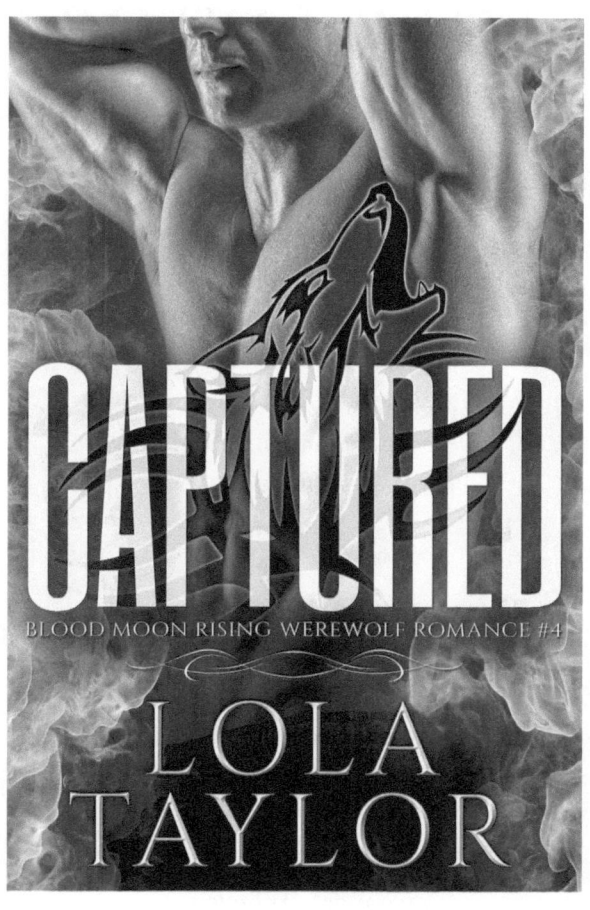

Read about Elijah and his mate in *Captured*, now available.

# OTHER BOOKS BY
# LOLA TAYLOR

The Her Dark Desires Trilogy
*Carnal* (free for a limited time!)
*Sinful*
*Soulful* (coming soon!)

Blood Moon Rising
*Fever* ( free for a limited time!)
*Protector*
*Betrayal*
*Captured*
*Sacrifice*
*Ritual*

Blood Moon Rising companion novels
*Lust*
*Forever* (coming soon!)

Standalone novels
*Shatter*

For a full list of titles, please visit
www.lolataylorbooks.com.

For more information, please visit
www.lolataylorbooks.com

Your opinion matters—please leave a review!

Thank you for reading my book! If you have a moment, I'd really appreciate an honest rating and review. They help authors stand out in a busy marketplace, plus they give browsing readers the nitty-gritty on books they're shopping. Everyone wins when you rate and review, so please do! Your opinion counts!

# ABOUT THE AUTHOR

"Lola Taylor" is a pen name created for the romances I can't show my grandma without blushing. My favorite genre to write is romantic suspense, usually involving hot werewolves, warlocks, or any other type of paranormal creature. Keep the action hot and the romance hotter—that's my motto! I'm a horror film junkie, I still love Halloween as an adult (seriously, I think I get more excited for it than some kids do), and what precious spare time I have is spent with my family, reading (everything from sci fi to middle grade), playing the flute, painting pretty pictures, or screwing around on Pinterest or Etsy. Hailing from the South, I currently live in the Midwest with five fur babies and my hubby.

You can connect with me on Facebook (www.facebook. com/lolataylorbooks) or my email (lolawritespnr@gmail. com). Learn more about me and my books at www. lolataylorbooks.com.